FINDING BALANCE

B. E. BAKER

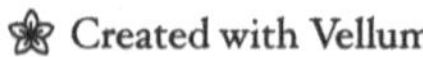 Created with Vellum

For Jocelyn

you can love your past and embrace your future
at the very same time <3

Plenty of things make me nervous. Math tests. Mean girls. Snarling dogs. Hospitals.

But singing doesn't.

Cuz I'm really good at it.

I don't mean that in a braggy way. I just like to do it, and people smile a lot when I do. But that's why I know I'm doing a good job singing *"Tomorrow"* for Mrs. Tassain, my music teacher—because she beams at me pretty much the whole time.

Even so, when she says, "Amy, I think you'd be the perfect person to play Annie in our second grade play," I'm surprised.

Shocked, really.

And then I'm scared.

Because Piper wants that part. Everyone knows she wants it. She practices the songs over and over, all the time. On the playground, at lunch, on class breaks. Whenever.

Twenty minutes ago, I heard her telling Mia and Lacy that the part is as good as hers. That's why I'm happy that the only other person in this room right now is Coach Brian. It would be just as bad if Piper knew I'd been offered Annie as if I took it, I think, but I doubt Coach Brian, who's directing the play, or Mrs. Tassain, who's handling the music, will tell anyone else.

Piper already hates me. The last thing I need to do is take her part. I can't even imagine what else she would do or say, but I know it would be bad. Really, really bad.

I shake my head pretty hard. "I don't want to play Annie," I lie.

Mrs. Tassain leans back in her chair, her eyes wide. "You don't *want* to play the lead role?"

"I mean, thank you so much, but no thank you."

She opens her mouth and then closes it. Mom does that sometimes when she's not sure what to say.

"I do want to be in the play, just not as Annie."

Mrs. Tassain taps her lip. "I suppose you could play Grace, the woman who is Mr. Warbucks' assistant."

And pretend to love Piper and tell her she's so great? Um, that would not be easy.

"What role would you like?"

What role won't make my life harder? "What about the mean lady? What's her name again?"

Coach Brian laughs. "You want to play Mrs. Hannigan?" His eyebrows shoot up. "Really?"

"She gets to boss everyone around, and I like to do that."

Mrs. Tassain snorts.

"Mom says I'm pretty good at it." I glance from Coach Brian to Mrs. Tassain, who are both smiling in kind of a painful looking way. "I have a little brother," I explain.

They both start laughing really loud. They must both have little brothers. They definitely get it.

"Well, if you're sure." Coach Brian writes something down on his paper.

"Does that mean I'm playing Mrs. Hannigan?"

Mrs. Tassain shrugs. "If that's what you want, then yes."

I'm smiling when I walk out the door. I should have known better.

"Why are you so happy?" Piper's slumped against the wall outside the music room waiting for her turn to sing, but she stands up and tosses her shiny brown hair over her shoulder.

It's too late, but I frown instead. "I'm not happy."

One of her eyebrows rises and she frowns back. Her best friends Lacy and Mia stand up too, and they take their places on either side of her. "I hope you don't think you're going to be Annie."

Lacy and Mia laugh.

"Because Mrs. Tassain would never pick someone who screams like a sheep."

"Bleats," I say, without thinking. "Sheep don't scream. They bleat."

Piper's lip curls.

Oh no.

"I better go," I say. "I'm sure my mom is waiting for me."

"Your mom's having a baby soon, right?" Piper presses her lips tightly and cocks one hip.

I nod.

"I figured she was, since she looks like a whale."

"She's really pretty," I say, even though I ought to just walk away. I ignore a lot of stuff she says to me, but I can't let Piper make fun of my mom.

"Are you worried?" Her voice sounds concerned, which scares me. A lot. Piper's never nice, not to me.

"About what?" I shift my backpack on my shoulders, a little nervous. My first mom died having my little brother, Chase. But Dad and Mom both say she's fine. "Her doctor is really good."

Piper rolls her eyes. "Not about that, dummy."

I wish she'd just say whatever mean thing she's going to say. "What then?"

"Well." She steps a little closer and pretends to whisper, but it's what Mrs. Tassain would call a stage whisper, which means everyone in the hall can still hear her. They all lean toward us, eager to hear what she'll say next. "Once she has a *real* kid, are you worried she won't like you anymore?"

I wasn't. Not until right now.

Mary hasn't known me a super long time, but she loves me. I know she does. I mean, I *know* she loves me. She can't fake smiling at me or tucking me in and kissing my forehead. Right? I'd know.

But for the first time, I wonder whether she loves me because I'm all she has. Will she love the new baby *more?* And if she does, what does that mean for me? Or for Chase?

Piper's smile gets bigger. Crap. I should have said something, or denied it, or anything but blinking and staring.

"My mom will love us all the same." But I don't sound very sure.

Probably because I don't feel very sure.

I turn on my heel and run down the hall toward the front of the school. The good news is that I push through the front door fast enough that no one in the hall sees me crying.

The bad news is that I'm wiping tears off my face when I push through the front door, and my dad is waiting for me in his giant truck—staring right at me when I come out, actually. Which means he definitely sees, and there's pretty much no way he's going to let this go.

He leaps from his truck, its engine rumbling loudly, and picks me up with both arms, hugging me tightly. "What's wrong, button?"

"Hello?" Mom's voice calls from inside his truck. "Luke? Are you still there?"

She must've been talking to him on the phone while he waited.

"He's hugging Amy," Chase yells. "We're all here."

"Uh, hang on one second," Dad whispers to me. "Chase is right. I'm here, but Amy's upset. Can I call you back?"

"Keep me on!" she practically shouts. "I want to know what's wrong!"

Oh, no.

"It's nothing," I say. "I fell and bumped my knee."

Dad opens the back door of the truck and tosses me up into the seat. He glares. "She's saying she fell, but she looks fine, and I think she's making it up."

I roll my eyes. "There's a girl who isn't being really nice, but it's fine. If you do anything, it'll make her be meaner."

"Can I talk to you about it when I get home?" Mom asks. "I'm on my way right now." She goes in to work ridiculously early so she can pick us up from school. Usually.

"What's wrong?" Chase asks. "Piper's a jerk still?"

"Is that her name?" Dad asks. "Piper?" His hand clenches and his lips press into a flat line. "Because I've got a few things to say to her parents."

"Dad!" Ugh. Today keeps getting worse. "Please leave it alone."

"Let me talk to Amy about it," Mom begs. "There's no reason to go around yelling at anyone's parents. Not yet, anyway."

"Fine," Dad says. "Fine." He finally climbs into the front seat of the truck, which is a good sign, but when he puts the shifter into the go position, the engine roars and the truck shoots forward awfully fast for a school parking lot. Which means he's still mad. "I'll see you soon, honey." There's a little beep when the call disconnects.

Yelling at Piper's mom is the worst thing they could do. I hope Mom listens to me. "I have good news," I say.

Maybe hearing about my part will make Dad happy enough to forget about the whole thing.

"What's that?" The fake happiness in his voice is super obvious, but it's better than growling.

"I got a part in the second grade play."

"*Annie*, right?" he asks.

I smile. He's listened to me practicing over the past few weeks. "Yep."

"That's great. Are you Annie?"

I look at my hands. Should I have taken that part? Will he be sad I'm not? "Uh, no. Not Annie."

"What part are you playing, then?"

"I'm going to be Mrs. Hannigan. I'm really excited."

"Isn't she the awful lady?" Dad turns around to look at me while we're sitting at a red light, his face surprised.

I grin. "Yes! I get to yell at everyone."

Chase says, "Awesome."

"And you're excited about that?" Dad searches my face.

I nod and force a smile. Hopefully he won't notice.

He turns back around and sighs heavily. "Well, if you're excited, so am I. Do you have practice every day after school, then?"

I pull the practice schedule out of my backpack and hold it on my lap. "If I was Annie I would, but I only have to go three days a week for Mrs. Hannigan. They set up the scenes so that we each come on the days we need to be there."

"That's smart."

"I'll give you the list of days when we get home."

"Well I'm very proud of you, Amy. You'll be amazing, and we'll all be there to see it."

I swallow. "The thing is, Mom is due to have the baby in April, right?"

Dad beams—which I can see in the rear view mirror. "Tax baby, due April fifteenth."

It's been a pretty common joke around our house lately. I'm not quite sure why that's funny, but I know it is. "Well, the play is on April seventeenth." I breathe in and out. "Can I still do it?"

Dad grunts. "Let me talk to Mary and I'll let you know for sure, but I think we can work something out. Even if the timing causes problems, I'm sure your grandma and grandpa can help."

"Okay."

When we get home, Dad starts unloading groceries. He must have taken Chase to pick up food while I was auditioning and then came back to get me.

Chase and I scramble inside as quickly as we can. Andromeda, our big shaggy white dog, licks our faces and hands. No matter how bad my day is, Andy's always super-duper happy to see me. I drop my backpack and sit on the floor to scratch her behind her ears. Chase throws his backpack down and flips his sneakers off, barely pausing on his way to grab a snack.

That kid always does the same thing.

Dad trips over a shoe and almost drops a gallon of milk. "Hey! Shoes, backpacks. What are we—"

"Animals?" I interrupt with a smile that isn't fake. He always says the same thing, but he never really seems angry.

I pick up Chase's shoes and backpack and carry it all over to the cubbies Mom had built after we moved here. "It's only a few feet away," I mutter, just like Mom does. "I'm not sure why it's so hard for them to put things away."

I love that I have a mom now, even when she complains. Even when she mutters. Even when she scowls. All the things that other kids complain about, I love. She does all those things because she loves me.

I just hope it doesn't change when she has a real kid, one that's actually hers.

The rumble of a garage door tells me she's home. My

heart speeds up. As if she knows I need it, Andy bumps my hand with her head, reminding me that she loves me no matter what. I sit on the shoe bench and resume scratching her ears. When Mom walks through the door, her face immediately lights up. "Amy."

"Hey."

She drops her purse and laptop bag on the bench next to me, hangs her keys on the hook, and crouches down in front of me, one hand going to her belly. After a half chuckle, she drops to the floor, cross-legged. "Wow, I am not coordinated right now."

I look at the big round part of her stomach where my new little baby brother is growing. I hope he loves me as much as I love him. And I hope Mom still loves me after he's born. "I think you're doing pretty good."

"Pretty well," she corrects. "So what's going on?"

She doesn't usher me into my room, or her room, or the family room. She drops down on the floor in the laundry room and immediately asks me what's wrong. Like I'm the most important thing in the world. For some reason, that makes me cry.

"Oh, no," she says softly. "What did I say?"

I shake my head.

But she pulls me down against her anyway, hugging me to her chest and stroking my hair. "I'm sorry. I didn't mean to upset you."

I shake my head.

"Look, we don't have to talk about it right now. But tell me this. Is there a girl at school who's being mean to you?" Her arms loosen enough for me to pull away and sit back on the bench.

I can't quite meet her eyes, but I nod.

"Okay. Is her name Piper? Is that what Chase said?"

I nod again.

"Well, this is the first I've heard about it, but I'm

guessing it's not a new problem, judging by your reaction and Chase's knowledge of her name."

My lip wobbles. When I finally look up, Mom's eyes are soft. She feels sorry for me.

"Oh, Amy. If you believe a single word I say, believe this. I may be older than you by quite a lot, but if there's one thing I know a lot about, it's having kids at school pick on me. It was a daily occurrence, and not a single adult ever did a thing about it. I handled it all on my own."

I think about that while Mom and Dad make dinner. Mom doesn't talk about when she was a kid very much, but since we never see her parents, I am thinking the stories aren't going to be very good. Aunt Trudy makes weird jokes sometimes too—like once she mentioned that they were raised by wolves. At least, I thought it was a joke because Mom laughed, but I'm not sure quite why it was funny.

Maybe she'll actually have some ideas that could help me. Maybe she'll understand why Dad can't go yell at Piper's mom.

When Mom starts to mix up the salad, I know it's almost dinner time, so I leave to wash my hands. When I come back out, I realize Mom and Dad are talking, and they don't sound very happy. Sometimes they do that. They wait until me and Chase aren't in the room to talk. Usually it's when they have something angry to say.

I worry they're talking all weird and snappy because of me, so I listen in from behind the half wall.

"It's a huge mistake, but it's not your fault," Dad says. "You didn't make the error."

"No I didn't, but he works for me, and as the boss—"

"But you didn't want to hire him, and when he screwed up last time, you demanded they let him go." Dad throws the kitchen towel at the countertop. "If they'd have listened to you, it wouldn't have happened."

Mom puts a hand on his shoulder. "We all answer to

someone, and it was still my job to make sure he didn't ruin anything else."

"I'm not mad at you." Dad leans toward her. "You know that, right?"

Mom smiles, her hand brushing his cheek. "Of course I do."

"But with our surprise baby coming at tax time, and this catastrophe with the filing, and Trudy and Paul getting married at Easter." He groans. "I'm already worried about you." He puts both his hands on Mom's belly. "I don't want you stressed out. Surely you understand why."

Mom kisses him, and it makes me smile. They may shout sometimes, but they do love each other. "You want to slay all my dragons and vanquish all my demons. I know, and I love that about you. But I can slay my own dragons, and you're strong enough and you trust me enough to let me."

"One of these days you're going to listen to me, and you're going to leave that dumb firm and start your own."

"With all the business I've brought in, I certainly could."

"And then you wouldn't be stuck hiring morons and cleaning up after their messes." Dad kisses Mom one more time. But the oven buzzes and they both spring into action. Mom pulls the rolls out, and Dad tosses croutons on the salad. Then they tell Alexa to announce that dinner is ready.

After dinner, Mom stands up and smooths her shirt over her stomach, tugging down on the bottom. "I think these shirts are shrinking," she says with a smile.

Dad laughs. "Yeah, they probably are."

I don't think they're shrinking. I think her belly is getting bigger. But maybe that's the joke.

Mom grabs the leash and Andy jumps to her feet. "I

thought Amy might want to go for a walk with me and Andromeda."

Andy rushes to Mom's side, patiently waiting while Mom fumbles to attach it to the hook on the collar.

"Okay." I tug my jacket on. It's not super-duper cold in Atlanta in March, but it's kind of cold, especially since the sun is getting low. And if I don't get my jacket, Mom will remind me, and then she'll have to wait while I get it. I may as well save us the time.

Will she still insist I wear a jacket after the baby is born? Maybe she'll be too busy to care.

We're not even past the edge of our yard, Andy pulling on the leash naughtily, when Mom says, "Now that you've had some time to think, and your dad and brother aren't looming over us, why don't you tell me what's going on?"

"What does 'looming' mean?"

She laughs. I love the sound of her laugh. It's like a fresh pile of leaves to jump into, and a fluffy pile of pancakes covered in syrup. "It means they're standing around, *watching* and listening and just..." She waves her hands, tugging on Andy's neck. "Being in the way."

"Oh."

She stops, the leash pulling tight. "Am *I* looming right now?" She crouches down again, her head at the same height as my shoulder. "You don't *have* to talk to me, just because I want to help. You can totally talk to your dad instead."

I swallow. She didn't say I could just not talk about it at all, which is what I want to do. "It's just that I don't think there's much anyone can do that won't make it worse."

"How about this." Her eyes stare into mine. "You tell me what's going on, and I *promise* that we won't do *anything* unless you approve it."

I blink. "But Dad—"

She takes my hand in hers. "Do you trust me to handle your father?"

I nod.

"Well, then. Tell me what's going on, and I'll make sure he abides by my promise. Deal?"

"Deal," I say.

And then I tell her.

❧ 2 ❧

AMY

Mom stands up and starts walking again, in her slow, kind of bouncy pregnant-lady walk, as if she knows it's easier for me not to have to tell her all this while she stares at me.

But her face hardens as I tell her the things Piper has said and done.

And I don't even mention any of what she said today, about her not loving me. I can't quite bring myself to say that out loud. I'm not sure I want to hear the answer. Because Mom's really good at almost everything, but she doesn't lie very well. If she tells me she'll love me exactly the same after the baby comes, I'll know whether she believes it.

Besides. She might not even know how she'll feel after the baby comes.

"You were offered the part of *Annie,* and you turned it down because you were worried what Piper might do or say about what?" Her knuckles turn white where they're holding the leash too tight. Dad's hands do that on the steering wheel when he's yelling at someone from work.

I think she's mad at Piper, not at me, but I'm not sure.

"I actually really want to play Mrs. Hannigan."

"That's not the point," she says, her eyes flashing. "You shouldn't—" She spins toward me, staring right at me. "I want to march into your choir teacher's office and tell her that you'd be the perfect Annie. In fact, if I could, I'd kick Piper right out of that school. Since I can't do that, I'd like to chew her out royally for being a brat." She sighs. "But I promised you that I wouldn't do anything you don't want me to do." Andy circles round and round her legs while she talks, and the leash gets tangled.

I take it from her and unwind it.

"Okay." Mom crouches down again, inspecting the cracks in the concrete to make sure there aren't any ants, probably. Then she collapses on the hard ground. "Sit."

I swallow, and then I sit. Andy sits next to me, her nose bumping against my face. It's nice to know people—and pets—care.

After being totally quiet for a minute, she almost whispers the words. "What do you want me to do?"

"I don't know," I say. "I just want her to stop being mean."

Mom laughs. "That would be nice, but usually objects in motion remain in motion until acted on by another force." She frowns then. "I haven't told you much about when I was a kid. She tucks my hair behind my ear. "That's because my mom left when I was really young. Close to your age, actually."

"She left?" My mouth dangles open. "Like, just went away? Or do you mean she died?"

Mom flinches. "No, she didn't die, sweetheart. She just got sick of being a mom, I guess, and she went away and never came back."

"I didn't know moms could do that."

She shakes her head. "Neither did I, at least, not until it happened to me."

I swallow. "Well. That stinks."

She nods. "It did, yes. And my dad didn't really step up like yours did. I think it broke him when she disappeared."

"I'm sorry," I say.

She puts her hand over mine, where I'm holding the leash. "I didn't tell you before because I didn't see the purpose in sharing it. But when I was your age, I didn't have nice clothes. I didn't have anyone to tell me to comb my hair. I didn't have shoes that fit."

So her life was way harder than mine. Now I feel bad for crying. I use my free hand to pick at a clump of tiny, bright green grass sprouts.

"Amy, I'm not telling you this so you'll feel sorry for me. I'm telling you this so that I can explain that when kids made fun of me, there wasn't anyone I could ask for help."

I glance back up at her. She doesn't look angry or like she thinks I'm a big baby either. "What did you do?"

"I got in fights sometimes." She smirks. "Pretty often, actually."

"Like—wait, did you punch people?" Because that would be so cool.

She laughs. "No, I didn't punch anyone. And I didn't really fight them for picking on me, but I did yell in a little boy's face when he made fun of Trudy. It didn't go well." She shakes her head. "I wish I'd had someone to offer me advice."

"What do you want to do?"

"One of the things I learned—mostly as an adult—was that if a kid is being mean, it's usually for one of two reasons. First, their parents are mean or have spoiled them, and they've learned to act poorly as a result. Or second, they're struggling with something really hard and their only way to deal with it is to make someone feel bad so they feel better."

Is she saying I should feel sorry for Piper? Or is she saying she's a brat? I frown.

"I know this doesn't sound great—for me to say that the little jerk's probably struggling. It might even make you feel bad for being angry. I'm not trying to do that, and I think you're absolutely entitled to all the things you're feeling. I'm feeling them, too. However, I also think it's easier to fix something when you know you're not the real problem." She touches my face gently. "But sadly, if her actions don't have anything to do with you, there may be no way for you to fix it, not alone."

"You want to let Dad yell at her mom?"

Mom shrugs. "I don't know. Maybe."

At least she's not lying, and she's listening.

"Or." She taps her lip. "I think if you let me talk to her mom and explain how she's been behaving, we might find out what's really going on in her life."

"No," I practically shout.

"Okay," she says. "It's okay." She pulls me in for a hug. "I wasn't kidding," she whispers in my ear. "I won't do anything you don't want me to do."

This time, I'm not embarrassed to be crying. And I believe her promise.

A squawking sound behind us shocks us both and Mom lets me go. "What the—?"

With my bawling like a baby, I forgot to hold Andy's leash. She ran off and is attacking some kind of bird, shaking it back and forth like a chew toy. I leap to my feet. "Andy! Stop!"

But she doesn't stop. It feels like it takes Mom two years to get to her feet and rush toward our dog. The second Mom reaches Andy's side, she drops the bird she was rattling.

It doesn't move. Or make any noise.

"Oh no." Mom hands the leash to me. "Hold her tightly."

I want to cry at the frustration in her voice. I wasn't holding Andy. That's why this happened. I let go of her leash, and now she's killed something.

"It's a chicken," Mom says. She bends over like she's going to pick it up.

"Wait," I say. "Dad wouldn't want—"

"You're right." Mom doesn't pause. "He would probably tell me not to touch it, but it's clearly domesticated." She picks it up gently. "And it's staring right at me, like it wants me to do something." She gulps and looks at the little blue house a few yards away. She walks slowly toward the front door and presses the bell, still cradling the poor bird's body against her belly.

It's still not moving.

The red door swings open. "Oh no," a woman wails. "Oh! What happened?"

Mom shakes her head. "I'm so sorry. My dog—she was on a leash, but I wasn't paying close enough attention and she managed to grab your chicken."

The woman's eyes fly wide. "Oh, no. Oh." She closes her eyes and whimpers.

"I am so, so sorry," Mom says again.

The woman breathes in and out and then opens her eyes again. "Well, it's kind of my fault too. She's an Andalusian, and they don't like to be confined. Usually she stays in my back yard, but she molted late and I forgot to trim her wings afterward."

"I think she might be..."

Mom passes her the bird and wipes her hands on her pants, smearing red across them. Gross.

The woman examines the limp grey bird carefully. "She's still alive, but I doubt she can survive a trauma of this severity." The woman sighs.

If I had been holding Andy, this wouldn't have happened. "It's all my fault," I blurt.

"No," Mom says. "It wasn't your fault at all, dear heart. It was mine. I'm the adult, and I shouldn't have let her leash go." She turns to the woman. "Please let me pay you for the chicken."

"I'm not even supposed to have them," the woman says. "The HOA doesn't allow it. I hope you won't report me."

Mom shakes her head. "I would never do that, but you have to let me pay you for her. I am truly sorry."

Pay for her, like she's already dead. But she's breathing. Even from here, I can tell her feathers are moving up and down. She's not dead. Not yet. "But maybe we could save her? Right? Maybe?"

The woman looks at me kindly, but there's no hope on her face. "Dog's mouths aren't very clean, and her back is pretty badly mangled. I worry that it would be a punishment to her to force any attempt at recovery."

Her words sink in slowly. "Wait." My mouth drops. "You're going to kill her?"

"It's probably the compassionate thing to do at this point," she says.

"It's not." I shake my head. "Maybe she won't die." We have to try at least.

"Amy, I'm sure—"

"We can't just give up on her."

"Unfortunately I'm an ER nurse," the woman says. "I'm working swing shift for the next week, so even if I wanted to try and save her, I don't have time to make sure she's eating and drinking, or to monitor that she's not suffering from an infection."

Mom's shoulders drop. She looks at me for a moment. "What if we did that?"

The woman's eyes widen. "You'd take a chicken?"

"I mean, I don't know much about them."

"You'd need to make sure she's drinking and eating. She can't just be left in the back yard. She'll need to be someplace warm and quiet."

"I think we could manage that." Mom glances at me. "The Mannings don't give up easily, do we Amy?"

I shake my head, my heart soaring. Maybe we can save her. Maybe I can fix this.

"If she doesn't eat on her own in the first day, you'll have to hand feed her," the woman says. "And that has to be done every two hours. Is that something you'd be willing to take on?"

"We'll figure it out," Mom says. "Because even when things are hard, we try to do the right thing."

I wonder whether she's talking about the chicken...or about Piper.

"My name is Lucy. I can give you my number and some chicken feed to last you at least a few days. I had a chicken survive a raccoon attack once—it lost an eye. The ordeal was terrible, but the recovery was much longer and harder than I anticipated. I doubt I'd have done it if I knew what I was getting myself into. I had to hand feed Alpha for weeks. And you'll want to give her plain yogurt for at least the first week. A dropper bottle or wide bore syringe is the best thing—"

"What about a kid's medicine dispenser?" Mom asks. "We have loads of those."

Lucy smiles. "That should work fine. Let me know your address and I'll bring some supplies down. But for now, you'll want to put her in a box lined with a towel or some newspapers or magazines."

Mom and Lucy discuss a few more details, and then Mom takes Andy from me, and Lucy puts the poor grey chicken in my arms. Its head flops against me, and it makes my heart hurt. It has soft, shiny feathers, except where Andy chewed them up. I walk about five feet behind Mom to make sure Andy keeps her distance. So far, she's curious, but not aggressive. I wonder why she attacked the bird before.

We're almost home before it occurs to me to worry that I might be covered in blood. Gross. I know Mom will do her best to clean it up, but I wish I wasn't wearing my favorite green shirt. "Hey Mom, do you think, if the chicken bled on my shirt, that you can get the stain out?"

"You call her 'Mom' now?"

Mom's head whips toward the street where Aunt Anica is standing, hand on her hip. Aunt Anica's frowning, but not at Mom.

She's frowning at me.

"Aunt Anica." I gulp. "Andy attacked a chicken on our walk. Now we're going to try and save it."

"We had no idea you were coming," Mom says sharply.

"I didn't realize I needed an appointment," Anica says, "but I'm sorry if I startled you. I meant to spend the night in Oklahoma City, but I decided to push through."

"Wait, did you drive here from San Francisco?" Mom asks. "Straight through?"

Anica nods. "And Mom and Dad aren't answering their phones or the door."

"They're on vacation," I say. "In Hawaii. They just left yesterday."

"Oh."

"I'm guessing you didn't tell them you were coming?" Mom asks.

"Not quite the surprise and excitement I expected," Anica says. "But I guess I did just show up without any warning. Actually, now that I think about it, I should probably just go find a hotel."

Mom glances back at me and my chicken, and her shoulders sag. "Don't be silly. I'm sure the kids will be delighted to have you stay with us. Please, come inside."

"Are you sure?" Aunt Anica and Mom stare at each other for a few moments. I'm not quite sure why.

Mom tosses her head toward the front door and Aunt Anica walks toward it. "So you're saving chickens now?" she asks, one eyebrow raised.

I squeeze the little gray bird gently. "I hope so."

Because if I'm not saving them, I'm killing them.

"I'll go put Andy in the backyard and have your dad set up a box in the garage," Mom says.

"Thanks. Good idea," I say.

Aunt Anica follows me around the corner and through the side door that leads into the garage. "Maybe I can help."

"Okay." I sit on a storage tub.

"Mary said to use a box, right?" Aunt Anica looks around, snagging a large box from the top shelf of a big black cabinet. "What about this?"

I nod. "Mom saves them for stuff like this."

"You rescue dying chickens often?" Aunt Anica half smiles.

I swallow. "No."

"Maybe raccoons? Snakes?" She looks at me expectantly.

"No, I mean, mostly we have them in case we need to carry big stuff or go to the mailbox. Mom's always prepared." I gulp when I realize I called her *Mom* again.

Anica sets the box on the ground and opens the flaps. Then she sits next to me on another storage tub. "You call her 'Mom.'"

"Yeah."

"When did that start?"

I shrug.

"You have a mom."

I blink.

"I'm surprised Mary lets you."

"Lets me?"

"Call her 'Mom,' when you've got a mom, a mom who loved you more than anything. She would still be here if she had any say in the matter."

She just got sick of being a mom and went away and never came back. That's what Mary said about her mom. But my mom didn't want to leave. She died. My words come out as barely a whisper. "Do you think Mom would be mad that I'm calling Mary 'Mom'?"

Aunt Anica places her hand on my knee. "I don't know. I can't imagine Lizzie ever being mad at you, no matter what you said or did, but I think it might hurt her feelings." Her head tilts. "Or maybe not. I'm not sure, since I can't really ask."

It hadn't occurred to me that Mom might be up in heaven looking down on me, frowning every time I use her name for Mary.

The garage door opens and Dad barrels through with an armful of towels. Mary's carrying two bowls.

"Anica, welcome," Dad says, his voice booming. "Always good to see you."

"Thanks, Luke. I appreciate you letting me stay."

"Of course, of course." He smiles at me. "Never a dull moment at Chez Manning. I hear we're commencing Operation Rescue Poultry?"

"I wasn't holding Andy's leash good enough," I say.

"Mary told me," he says. "And I agree with her assessment. It wasn't your fault, not even a little bit. Accidents happen. This goofy little bird was out when she shouldn't have been, and Andy took it upon herself to protect her two favorite people from a perceived threat. Even so, we're going to move heaven and earth to fix her up again, if that's what it takes."

"Thanks."

Dad spreads a towel across the box Anica opened, and I

set the chicken down inside. She fluffs up and lifts her head.

"Hey, she's perking up a little," Mary says.

"Maybe she wants something to eat or drink," I say.

She sets the bowls in the box next to her, but the chicken just settles on the towel and ruffles her feathers again before her head sinks down toward her chest.

"Well that's a dangit." I say.

"Lucy sent me some links and I read up on this a bit while your dad was grabbing the towels," Mary says. "If we press her beak into the water a little, she'll drink. It's an instinct. She needs to drink, especially if she is going into shock, which is common for chickens that have been injured. I dissolved aspirin into her water. Lucy told me how much would be an effective dose, but this little gal needs to drink about half of what's in that bowl for it to work."

"Okay." I feel guilty doing it, but I push her head gently into the water bowl. She lifts her head then, bobbing it up and around. "Hey, that worked. I think she was swallowing."

Mary smiles. "Oh, good. Now let's see if she'll eat any of these." Mary hands me another bowl with worms in it.

"Gross," I say. "What are these?"

"Lucy brought them with the crumbles. She says chickens love mealworms."

"What's this chicken's name?" I ask. "Did she mention that?"

Mary shakes her head. "She wasn't named. Lucy just called her the Andalusian."

Huh. "Well, you need a name, pretty lady." I stroke her head, and then I press it down toward the water again. "Once she drinks more, we can try worms."

"Smart," Aunt Anica says. "Water is the most important thing, if chickens really can go into shock."

"If Mary said so then it's true," I say.

Dad and Mary look at each other, and I realize that I called her Mary. I wait to see if anyone says anything about it.

No one does.

Not even after Aunt Anica goes inside. Mary sits with me and holds my hand while Dad cleans out the wound on the chicken's back, but she doesn't mention it. She's silent while she helps me get the water down the little bird's throat and while we hand feed her some mealworms. She's such a cute little grey chicken. Since she's eating a little on her own and drinking when I encourage it, I really hope she's going to be okay.

"Hope," I say. "I think we should name her Hope."

"That's a great name," Mary says. "This world can always use a little more hope."

I know I sure could. I figured my prayers before bed would be about Piper, but instead I decide to use them on Hope. If God only has time to help me with one thing, I'd rather save her than me.

But secretly, I hope He has time for both of us.

❧ 3 ❧

MARY

"I hate your sister-in-law," I say.

Luke laughs. "She's always been a bit of trouble-maker, but don't worry about it. It'll blow over, I'm sure."

"Amy has been calling me 'Mom' for a year, Luke. A year!" I sink into bed, my feet aching, my back throbbing, my head pounding. "Anica's here for five minutes, uninvited and unannounced I might add, and suddenly Amy's calling me *Mary*."

Luke slides into bed and pulls me against him, his hands working out the knots in my shoulders. "Today was a long day before she got here, which doesn't help. You're usually the one telling me to be patient with people. Speaking of patience, what did Amy say before Andy lost her mind and attacked that poor chicken?"

I close my eyes and sink back against him. "Basically what Chase did. There's a terrible spoiled brat named Piper who is making her miserable. I'm sure she's jealous of Amy's poise and intelligence, but it's hard to have perspective on that when you're so young."

"And?"

"I told her I would let her dictate how we handle it, and before you get upset at that idea, someone treating her this way is making her feel out of control. If we step in and handle things another way, it will only increase her unease and fear, believe me. I did put the idea in her head that this little girl is probably being rude because she's hurting or suffering in her home life. Amy's such a sweet girl, I imagine that knowing that will help."

Luke's hands freeze. "You're kidding, right?"

"About what?"

"You told her to bear up under the taunting with fortitude? You told her she should feel sorry for the bully?"

I frown. "That's not what I said. I told her I'd do whatever *she* wanted me to do, and I even suggested that Piper's mother and I should have a chat. I also offered to talk to the school. But I also explained that Piper is likely acting the way she is because Amy's life is better than hers. I gave her action options and insight—both can be helpful in making a decision about the way to proceed. What I don't want is for her to feel powerless because we barreled in and took over, in spite of her concerns we'd do just that."

"She is powerless," Luke says. "She's seven. That's why she has parents."

I spin around. "You think I handled it wrong."

"I think you're new to this."

"At being a human? At dealing with spoiled little girls? Or at handling conflict? Which of these things are new to me?"

"Whoa." Luke throws his hands up like he's defending himself from a tiger attack. "Easy. We're on the same team, remember?"

"Are we?"

He laughs then. "I love you so much, you crazy mama bear. You know that, right?"

"I might be a little hormonal," I admit. "A tiny bit."

"You think?" He smiles. "I would never have let her bring that chicken home. I think it's more stress than you can handle, and it's a risk. She's only going to get more attached and if the chicken lady—"

"Lucy," I say. "Her name is Lucy."

"Okay, but if Lucy, who knows a lot about chickens, thought she should be put down—"

"It was so brave of Amy to want to save her, and I think doing something can be therapeutic. Besides, she didn't think she should be put down, she just didn't have the time to commit to trying to save her."

"And neither do you." He eyes my stomach pointedly. "But that's fine. We can give both the chicken and the brat a few days to see which direction they head, but you need to consider that she may need a little more parental intervention than fierce, independent little Mary had at her age. You may have decimated your foes with a single stroke of your broadsword, but Amy's not exactly the same as you. And she doesn't *need* to be. She has us."

She's not the same as me. He doesn't say this, but it hangs in the air. *She's not even related to me.* In case I'd forgotten, that has been made very clear to me today. "I just hope you're not implying that I'm handling this differently because she's not my daughter. Because I would set this town on fire for her."

Luke wraps his arms around me and pulls me back toward his chest. "I know you would, and it may yet come to that. But for now, sheathe your horrifying claws. At least she opened up to you. That's a good thing."

I toss and turn half the night wondering whether I gave the right advice, and wondering whether I made a mistake with that dumb chicken.

When my alarm goes off at four-forty-five the next morning, I groan.

"Should I get up too?" Luke asks blearily.

I shove him back toward his pillow in answer. Why should we both suffer? I check on Hope before I leave for the day. She's listless, not even lifting her head when I come into the garage and turn on the lights. "Hey there, little chicken. You may not know this, but the little girl who insisted on bringing you here, well. She's had a rough life so far. Her mother passed away, and I think that may be part of the reason she needs you to survive this so badly. So I need you to really try, okay?"

Hope shows no understanding, possibly because she's a chicken and can't speak English. Or it could be that she's in pain and needs more aspirin water. After all, if my back was in constant agony, I wouldn't eat either. "Okay little girl. You're not going to like this, but I need you to drink more of this water."

It takes almost twenty minutes, but I get the aspirin water into her. I text Luke so he knows when I dosed her, the dosage amount, and when to redose.

Between the tax disaster Patrick made at work, general tax season chaos, this pregnancy, and Trudy's wedding, I did *not* need to add rehabbing a chicken to my list. But Amy needed it, and that comes first. Always. I just hope it doesn't die and break her heart. I'm worried Luke is right and that it was a mistake to let her bring this thing home at all.

After losing a mother, it felt like she was brave to want to save this chicken. But if she fails. . .

I shake off my concern and get in the car. Nothing to do about it right now. Which doesn't keep me from fretting all the way to the office. I spend the next two hours trying to find a way out of the mess Patrick made. When I finally find it, I want to break something.

I found a solution, but it's still going to cost LitUp an extra two hundred thousand dollars over the next three years.

For a mistake my firm made, which means we need to make the client whole for it.

I check the clock and decide that ten-thirty in New York is late enough that Peter might be in the office already. I dial his number, dread forming in my belly. The baby kicks just then—startling a smile out of me. "Be patient little guy. We have a few more weeks yet."

"Excuse me?" Peters voice booms, even through the receiver.

"Sorry," I say. "This is Mary Wig—Manning."

"Good morning, Mary."

"This isn't going to be a good call," I say by way of warning.

He shouldn't be surprised since his son is the one who made this mess, but he's still utterly silent while I walk him through what happened, including the erroneous election and the fiscal impact on our client. He didn't become the lead partner by accident. He immediately understands the ramifications. "You want to offer the client compensation."

"I do. In addition to being the right thing, it's also exactly what we'd do for any other client to whom we did this."

"But this is your husband's company, isn't it?" His voice is sharp.

"It is."

"That's a bit of a conflict of interest, I'd say."

"You didn't say that when I brought them in as an account. Their business alone is equal to a tenth of the Atlanta client roster." I can't believe he's insinuating that I'm trying to force the partnership to do something we wouldn't do for any other client.

"They weren't about to cost my firm two hundred thousand dollars when you asked to bring them on."

"They could sue us, and you know it. They'd win lawyer's costs, fees, and the same sum I'm requesting."

"Unless."

"Unless what?"

"You could convince your husband not to sue."

"Your son was responsible for the entire mess," I snap. "You and I both know it. So here's the bottom line, *Peter.* Your son will change offices at a minimum, since you seem unable to fire him, and you'll offer full restitution to LitUp. You have until Monday to let me know whether you'll comply with these terms."

"And if I don't?"

"I'll be severing my partnership with Frank & Meacham and starting my own firm. And I'll be sure that every single partner knows exactly why."

"Your optional maternity leave starts next week. Are you positive you want to toss this grenade onto the pile right now?"

I plan to work up until the day I have the baby, but I lined up an assistant manager for the office just in case the baby comes early. It's the responsible move, especially right around tax time. "If you think I'm any less likely to go to war because I'm pregnant, then you don't know me at all." I hang up.

But my hands are both trembling, and when Margaret comes in, I stand up. "Do you feel capable of taking over for me today?"

Margaret's steel grey eyes widen. "Will you be available by phone?"

"Of course."

Some of the tension leaves her body. "Then yes, I think so. I thought you meant to be here until Monday."

"It's nearly eleven am," I say. "I arrived here at five-thirty. I think that counts as a half day at the very least, don't you?"

She doesn't argue.

Which is good. Normally the thought of firing someone wrecks me, but today? Today I'd like to do it. Not her, though. Margaret has been a true godsend. "I'll finish reviewing all the reports from last week and send my approvals once I get home. I'll also review those letter rulings Jonathan sent, and if you have any issues, definitely call me."

"Thanks," she says. "That will be perfect."

"See you tomorrow."

She bobs her head and I shuffle out of the office. If my stomach gets any bigger, I'll need to roll out of here on a scooter. Actually, a scooter would probably be an epic fail. I'm so uncoordinated right now that I'd probably flip and kill myself.

When I get home, I've got a text from Lucy. I HAVE A LITTLE TIME BEFORE I HAVE TO LEAVE FOR MY SHIFT. CAN I COME BY AND CHECK ON THE CHICKEN NOW?

I text back. YES. AMY NAMED HER HOPE, FYI.

I'M SO GLAD SHE'S STILL HANGING IN THERE.

Hearing that Lucy is relieved that she didn't die overnight isn't very heartening. I cross the garage to the box, disappointed to see the food untouched and the chicken sitting completely still in a huddle in the corner, right where I left her. The poop behind her is runny and has soaked into the towel. I'm not sure whether that's good or bad.

Lucy knocks on the front door almost the second I walk inside the house. Andy barks and barks and barks. "Hush, girl." I pat her head and open the door. "Thanks for coming by," I say.

"Of course," Lucy says. "I'm happy to come by as often as you need."

"You might think it's a little odd that, knowing nothing

about chickens, we decided to try and save her." I gesture for Lucy to come inside.

She follows me to the garage. "Everyone reacts a little differently to things like this. Even people in the chicken world vary pretty widely. Some would put her down and some would wait and see if she dies." She pauses in the doorway between the house and garage. "Very, very few are willing to take on hand feeding and whatnot. So if it's too much, no one would blame you." She looks down at my stomach. "Especially right now."

I sigh. "Since Amy's at school, I can explain that her mother passed away a few years ago, and I think that may be why she was so desperate that we try and save Hope. It's also the reason I was reticent to turn her down."

Lucy's eyes widen. "Oh, no. I'm so sorry to hear that." Her eyes soften. "And now I'm really concerned about Hope's chances." She gestures toward the side storage area. "Is she in the box?"

I nod. "What do you think her odds are?"

Lucy takes a moment to look Hope over and then shrugs. "It's hard to know, but with a dog bite that looks as nasty as that one. . ."

Not good, I take it.

She lifts Hope from the box to inspect her, and then sprays on more Vetericyn.

"Oh." I can't quite help exclaiming. "Look!" Beneath where Hope had been sitting, there's a white egg.

Lucy smiles. "Looks like she laid."

"That's good news, right?" I lean over and pick it up.

"Not really. It's probably the last one she'll lay for a very long time. It takes about 24 hours for their bodies to make an egg, so this would have been formed before the attack yesterday. Her body's just purging it, so don't read much into it."

Dang.

"She's lethargic." Lucy sets her back in the box, shifting the food so it's in her easy line of motion. "Has she been eating on her own?"

"She ate a few worms last night."

"Since then?"

I shake my head. I'm terribly afraid Luke was right. I should have held firm and let Lucy deal with this poor sweet little girl.

"If she doesn't eat soon. . ."

"Luke told me he picked up plain yogurt. It's in the fridge, in case that helps."

"I feed mine yogurt pretty regularly, and it's a treat. Maybe it'll be the motivation she needs."

I bring a bowl out, but Hope doesn't move. If anything, she looks more exhausted from her medical exam.

"You've been dosing her with aspirin water?"

I nod.

"Well, at this point, we have two ways we can go. Chickens don't have a strong drive to live, like humans or even dogs or cats might. If she's not eating, it's unlikely she will start on her own."

"What do you mean, on her own?" I gulp.

"Well, my chicken that survived that raccoon attack. . ." Lucy sighs. "I force fed her for almost two months."

"Two months?" My hands go unconsciously to my belly. "I can't do that."

Lucy's lips compress, but not in judgment. She gets it. "I don't have time either."

"Amy—"

"She's probably too young to do it herself. It's pretty frustrating and requires a significant amount of coordination. Here, I can show you." She crouches down. "To do it right, you need to hold her head like this." She places her palm at the base of the back of Hope's head. "You force her beak open with your free hand and hold it in place, then use a syringe to squirt yogurt or a spoon to put softened feed pellets in her mouth."

"But will she swallow?"

"Luckily that's a reflex. But you have to feed her about every two hours during the day, since their crops can only process so much at a time."

"Crops?" It's confusing. And the whole thing leaves me very defeated.

Lucy touches her throat. "The crop is a sack at the bottom of her throat. It sort of regulates how much food their stomach can get at a time so they don't overload. But if you overfill the crop from force feeding too much, she can get a sour or impacted crop."

Great. I could kill her trying to save her. Lucy's right. This is too much. I open my mouth to tell her never mind. Maybe she'll still deal with it.

But then I look down at Hope's sweet little face, her dove grey feathers so soft. And I think about Amy, her tender heart yearning to fix this. It's not her fault—if anything, it's mine—but she thinks it's hers.

Force feeding a chicken every two hours would be. . . moronic. More than I can handle. Too much. And yet, I find myself asking Lucy to show me how much Hope should be eating, and how exactly to give it to her. Twenty minutes later, I've fed Hope her first meal of yogurt and aspirin water and a little pellet mash. It was messy and frustrating. My back hurts and my hands are trembling, but my heart has expanded.

Nothing that's worth anything in life is easy.

"I better go," Lucy says.

"Thank you," I say. "I'll go by the feed store and see whether I can buy everything on the list you made. Without your help, we wouldn't have a chance."

Lucy's face is kind. "Without me breaking the HOA rules, you wouldn't be in this situation. I'm really sorry about that too. I feel like I've made your life much harder. Maybe I should've said no."

I smile at her. "Decisions when kids and pets are involved are hard. What I wouldn't give for a crystal ball."

"For what it's worth, it really looks like you're doing a lovely job of filling some pretty big shoes."

The second I close the door, tears pour down my face. She has no kids herself, and she hasn't seen more than a moment of our lives—she's hardly an expert on the kind of job that I'm doing with Amy and Chase. But the fact that she thinks I'm doing a good job helps more than it should. I think, even with my reservations, I wasn't prepared for quite how hard it is to be a parent.

You never know if you're making the right decision.

You worry constantly.

And you never get a break. Never.

But being Amy and Chase's mother means more than anything else I've ever done.

I'm struck at the same time by complete bafflement that my mother could ever leave us and unwelcome insight into Peter's reticence to let me fire his idiotic son. But denying our children the right to experience the consequences of their actions—denying them experience with real life—it's no favor.

Which is why I'm going to fight for this little chicken with all I've got and if she dies, Amy and I will face that together. My resolve is firm when I go back inside.

"Morning," a groggy voice says from the other side of my open fridge door.

I startle. I had completely forgotten that Anica was staying with us. Yet another delightful addition to my life. "Uh, good morning." I glance at the clock. I've been up for nearly eight hours, and she's just rolling out of bed? I shove my judgment down very deep. "Let me know if you have trouble finding something to eat."

"Coffee. All I need is coffee."

I point at the cabinet where we keep the instant coffee. "Check there. Or if you want to make a pot, that's fine too." I point at the coffee maker.

"Thanks." Anica half-frowns. "I figured you'd be at work."

Did she wait to get up until she thought we'd all be gone? If so, why bother visiting at all? "Been there and now I'm back again. I have a chicken here to care for, after all." I don't mention that I threw down the gauntlet at work, telling my boss I'd be quitting soon. It's not really any of her business.

"A chicken?" Anica lifts both eyebrows. "You're skipping work for a chicken? Aren't you like the boss of some huge law firm?"

Again, I stifle my irritation. I've explained that I'm a CPA several times, but I guess it hasn't stuck. "Accounting firm," I say. "And normally I wouldn't have been able to take a half day like this, but as I've been transitioning to prepare for the baby, I have support staff in place."

"That's handy," Anica says.

"Handy?" What does that mean?

"Well, it lets you swoop in like a knight in shining armor to save that chicken."

Shining armor? Like I'm some usurper—an outsider saving her niece. My nostrils flare and my heart speeds up in my chest, but I will not let her upset me. Once I have my irritation in check, I say, "Speaking of, I better head to the feed store. I only have a few hours until I need to pick up Chase and Amy from school."

"Right." Anica starts to brew a pot of coffee. A whole pot—she either plans to drink an awful lot, or she's a little too good for instant coffee.

What's wrong with me? I never drink instant either.

I shake my head. Clearly this pregnancy and work

drama is making me defensive and crabby when I should be opening my heart. This poor woman lost her sister to something outside of anyone's control and watching me here with her brother-in-law and children, well, it probably feels to Anica like her sister has been replaced. That can't be a great experience. "Well, if you need anything." I scribble my name and number on a notepad. "Feel free to text me."

"Or I can text Luke." She leans against the counter and crosses her arms.

I grit my teeth. This woman could be awarded an honorary PhD in annoying me. How does she do it so effortlessly? "Sure, that's fine too."

"What time will the kids be back?"

Ah. She wasn't avoiding me so much as making it clear that she's here for them, not for me or Luke. That's fine. I don't even mind. They're all she has left of her sister. It makes sense. "Usually about three-thirty, depending on how long the pick-up line takes. Amy will have practice for her musical tomorrow, but today's her day off."

"She's in a musical?"

I smile. "She's playing Mrs. Hannigan in *Annie*."

"That's a pretty sexist play," Anica says.

I step toward Anica, my hand gripping the countertop tightly. "If you breathe a word of criticism to Amy about the play or her part in it," I say, "you will not be welcome in this home. Are we clear?"

"You can't kick me out of Luke's house," Anica says.

"Oh." I laugh, but it's bitter. "I think you'll find that I can. Besides. Technically, this is *my* house. It was a gift from my husband when he proposed. He put it in my name, and it remains that way."

"Wow, no shock that you fell for him. A guy who can gift you a house like this." She tilts her head, casually implying that I'm a gold digger.

"You don't know anything about me, Anica, and if you think Luke has such poor taste, then you don't know him very well."

A smile spreads slowly across Anica's face. "You're mad that I gave Amy a hard time about calling you 'Mom.'" Her lips twist, but in a satisfied way. As though she knows she's dealt me a harder blow than any I could possibly deal her.

And she's right.

"It doesn't matter to me what Amy calls me," I lie. "What matters is whether she feels valued and loved, and I believe she does."

"Lizzie didn't sing," Anica says. "And I didn't realize that Amy did either. Guess that's something you're encouraging."

"I can't even carry a basic tune, but Luke sings almost as well as Amy," I snap. "She sings anything and everything she hears, and she's delightful at it. So yes, I encourage it. I encourage anything that fills her heart with joy, as should you—because that little girl deserves every bit of happiness available." I've said too much, but I can't seem to stop. "You should examine your words before you say them in the future." I purse my lips. "Consider whether you're helping Amy, or just trying to hurt someone else. In case you can't recall what I'm sure your mother taught you, doing things to harm others is *bad*."

I spin on my heel and head for the garage, spurred onward by my righteous indignation.

Every ounce of outrage whooshes out of me when I notice Hope in the corner of her box. Her light grey head is slumped against the towel, face down, beak turned sideways. Thankfully she's still breathing, but when I check the wound to reapply the Vetericyn Lucy gave us. . . maggots are squirming around in the open wound. I stifle a shout and yank my hand back.

As a pregnant woman, my gag reflex is already pretty

sensitive, so it's hardly surprising that this bumps me over the top. Thankfully, Luke carried a whole stack of towels into the garage last night, and I had a small breakfast. It's relatively easy to clean up.

I text Lucy. HOPE'S SLUMPED DOWNWARD, BARELY BREATHING. AND I NOTICED MAGGOTS IN THE WOUND.

She doesn't text back while I'm driving to the feed store, and she hasn't texted by the time I've gathered the supplies on her list. The three employees I ask don't seem to know anything about chickens, so they're useless. Thankfully, as I'm approaching the register, Lucy finally replies. She sends several links to articles, and a short message. SHE NEEDS ANTIBIOTICS OR SHE'S A GONER.

Unfortunately, penicillin is on back order at three different places, and I'm running out of time to search.

NO PENICILLIN ANYWHERE. SOME KIND OF RUN ON ANIMAL ANTIBIOTICS OR SOMETHING.

I glance at the clock. I need to leave in the next twenty minutes or I'll be late to pick up Amy and Chase, and Luke has a meeting—he can't do it. The idea of taking Amy home to see Hope circling the drain without a plan for how to help her makes me want to puke again.

As if she can sense my complete and utter failure, Lucy's name lights up on my phone. Embarrassingly, I'm bawling when I answer. "Hello?"

"Mary? Are you alright?"

"I can't just let her die, but I can't find any penicillin! I'm such a failure." I hiccup. So much for her not realizing what bad shape I'm in right now. If I can't handle a chicken, how will I survive a baby?

"I'm thinking you might be upset over more than just Hope," Lucy says.

She's right. I've got an unwelcome step-sister-in-law—is

that the right title? A third-trimester pregnancy. A mess at work. And a daughter being bullied by a spoiled brat at school.

"You're right. This has definitely not been my week."

"Okay, well, have an employee walk you down the aisle and tell me what other antibiotics they have—and make them check everywhere. There should be a few that don't require refrigeration. I imagine they'll have something we can use, even if it's a Hail Mary."

Somehow, she's able to stay on the phone while we review the refrigerated medicine, which is a bust, and then go down another aisle for cattle. "Noromycin?" Lucy stops me. "What does it say beneath the brand name?"

How does she know it's a brand name? I look lower on the bottle. In parenthesis below the bright blue lettering, there's a long word. "It says 'oxytetracycline injection.' Does that help?"

"Ah, yes. We can use that. It'll have to be a super tiny dose, but let me look it up. Can you send me a screenshot? Luckily swing shifts are extra nurses for when things are at their worst—but today's not too busy, so I have time to look at this. If it stays slow, I can probably break away in time to come check on Hope after dinnertime tonight. I'll bring some syringes and do the first injection so you can do the rest."

A shudder passes through me at the thought of poking that poor little bird and shoving chemicals into her broken little body. But the maggots. Ugh. "Okay," I say. "Thanks."

I'm not entirely sure Hope will survive that long, but I pay another $20 for medicine for this longshot anyway.

"You said this is for a chicken?" The lady with a side ponytail at the register pops her gum.

I nod and hand her the money.

"You know chickens cost like, less than five bucks, right?"

"I didn't know that," I say. "But it's not about the money."

One of her eyes scrunches up and her mouth turns up into a forced smile. "Okay. Whatever. But you could buy, like five new chicks for the same price as this stuff." She points at a big metal trough, and I realize it's peeping. There must be chicks inside.

Not the point. "All life has value," I say. "And we're going to try and save this one."

She doesn't argue with me anymore, which is good. I'm not sure I can really justify my actions at this point.

At least Amy chose a good name for the chicken. I might never have hoped for anything as much as I hope that dumb chicken is alive when Amy and Chase and I get back home from school.

Somehow, she is. Barely breathing, but still alive.

Darling, sweet Amy insists on using tweezers to pick out the maggots one by one while I try not to puke again. No matter what Luke, Anica, or I say, nothing lures Amy in to eat dinner. "I'm not leaving Hope until she's gotten her medicine," she insists.

When Lucy arrives, she laughs about the maggot removal. Her voice is kind at least when she says, "As gross as they look, maggots are fly larvae, and they only eat dead and infected flesh. So they're not actually doing much damage. They're just an indicator that something is wrong. Which is good—that's one of the main ways your mom knew Hope needed antibiotics."

"Thank you for coming over." Amy beams at Lucy.

"You're welcome," Lucy says graciously. I can tell she's already pretty fond of Amy.

"I hope your family isn't mad we keep calling you over here." Amy looks at her shoes.

Lucy laughs. "I'm not married, and I live alone. That's why I work so much, and it's also why I didn't think I could do this." She gestures at Hope. "I know it may not feel like it, but you're really giving Hope her best chance. I'm impressed by how much you and your mother have been willing to do for this darling little chicken. She's a very lucky little girl."

"Why aren't you married?" Amy asks.

Oh, no. "Amy, we don't—"

"It's okay," Lucy says. "I wish adults would approach things as simply and as forthrightly as children." She brushes her hands on her scrub pants. "I haven't met a single guy yet who cared more about helping other people than themselves." She shrugs. "If you find a guy like that, you send him my way, alright?"

Amy nods seriously, like she's going to find Prince Charming for Lucy from her wide pool of options as a second grader. "I will."

I don't laugh, but it's hard. "What about feeding her?" I ask. "I wasn't sure what to do. She hasn't eaten since noon when you showed me how to feed her, but shoving food down her throat now seems. . ." I shake my head. "Mean, maybe."

"She won't be able to swallow when she's like this, I imagine." Lucy strokes Hope's neck and back like Amy has been doing. "She's too zapped. But if this tetracycline does its job, she'll perk up quite a bit tomorrow, and she'll need really consistent meals."

She doesn't say anything else for which I'm grateful, but I hear it in her voice.

She'll either perk up by tomorrow morning, or Hope will be dead.

❧ 4 ❧

LUKE

When I finish reading Chase his bedtime story and walk back into the living room, Anica's flipping through channels on the TV like her finger is broken and it's stuck pressing the channel up button.

"Everything okay?"

She drops the remote. "You scared me."

I sink onto the seat at the end of the sectional and turn toward her. "I can't help the fact that I move with the agility of a jungle cat."

Anica rolls her eyes. "In some ways you haven't changed a single bit."

"In some ways?" I pat my belly. "Are you saying I've gained weight?"

She arches one eyebrow. "Hardly."

I lean forward, resting my elbows on my knees. "What's going on, Anica? What's with the surprise visit and poking the bear?"

"Are you likening your new wife to a bear?"

"She's a pregnant woman. They're all crabby—your sister was too."

Anica whistles. "Don't let Mary hear you talking about her or you might get mauled."

"Mary's a miracle in my life," Luke says. "And you of all people should understand that."

Anica snorts. "She's currently skipping out on work to doctor a chicken."

I straighten. "She's helping *your niece* with something that matters to her. And Mary has never skipped out on a moment of work in her life. She shifted the timing in which she accomplished her job to accommodate what matters more to her." I can't quite contain the fury. "Not that it's any of your business, but you couldn't ask for a better mother to your niece and nephew, and she had no role model to help her learn that."

"My niece and nephew don't need a new mom." Anica's eyes flash. "They have a mother."

"They do not. Elizabeth died." A frog always creeps up my throat when I talk about her, making it hard to speak. "Losing her broke me, and those children paid for that. Do you really think she wants us all to suffer forever? Should we beat ourselves nightly? Is that what you do?"

"Don't be stupid," Anica says.

"Why? Because you've cornered the market on that particular behavior?"

"Amy calls Mary '*Mom*', like she's totally forgotten about Lizzie. Like she never existed." A tear rolls down Anica's face and my anger evaporates.

"I miss her too," I say. "It hits me at odd times, you know. Like when I see a cardinal. Or when I pass cotton candy at the county fair."

"Lizzie loved cardinals," Anica whispers. "She used to sketch them, you know, when she was younger."

I nod.

"And she made herself sick on cotton candy, every time." She smiles. "It was like she couldn't stop eating it."

"I'm aware."

"But she's more than a few funny quirks that you can trot out like a party anecdote," Anica says. "And it's like the other stuff." She chokes. "It's like the stuff that made her who she is. . .it's like it's evaporating." She looks at the ceiling. "When she first died, I could hear her voice in my mind. I knew just what she'd say, but now, it's like I don't know anymore, like I'm forgetting who she really was."

Anica drove out here without calling her parents. She *drove,* not flew, like she's not planning to go back any time soon. Instead of yelling at her, instead of picking the fight I desperately want to pick, I stuff down my anger. I do it for the little sister who doggedly loved and supported my wife. I do it for the woman Elizabeth admired—not for the broken woman stirring up trouble in my living room. In memory of who she really can be, I shove my rage down and force myself to be kind when I say, "Why are you here?"

She wrings her hands in her lap, staring intently at her fingers. "I can't write. Not a single word."

"What does that mean?" How can that be? I thought she just put out a book?

"I wrote a book the year after Lizzie died. I thought it was my best work—and my publisher dutifully released it."

"And?"

"That was four and a half years ago, Luke."

"Wait." Could it have been that long? I guess I wasn't paying much attention to anything, and then I was so in love. . . Have I really failed to take care of Anica this epically?

"That book I vomited out bombed, as it should have. It's terrible. I didn't even earn back my advance. My publisher dropped me, and when I didn't write anything else in two years, my agent did too." When she finally meets my eyes, I notice that hers are shattered, haunted, broken.

How was I so self-absorbed that I missed her flailing? After Elizabeth died, I was drowning myself, that's how. "How have you been paying your bills?"

She laughs. "You're assuming I *have* been paying them."

"If you need money—"

She shakes her head. "I've been lucky enough to get a substantial royalty check twice a year still, but it's smaller each time. It wasn't enough to cover all my expenses, so I started waitressing. At first I thought it might inspire me, you know? Give me something to do, force me to get out of bed, the whole starving artist thing was almost romantic as a bump in the road." She picks at her nails. "But then I sort of just fell into this routine."

"You should have told me," I say.

"People who need help can't ask," she says. "Isn't that the irony of it?"

It may be the truest thing she's ever said. She may not be writing, but she still commands language adeptly. "So what brought you here?"

"The restaurant I worked at closed. After it went under, I was getting ready to apply for jobs at other restaurants and when I looked at my resume, it hit me. I had been an author—a two time New York Times bestselling author. My career was going somewhere—all my dreams were coming true."

She closes her eyes.

"But I realized that I'm not an author anymore. Waitressing is perfectly respectable, but it wasn't what I wanted. It wasn't my goal, or my dream, or my calling. Nevertheless, it had become my life. Suddenly I could only think about my life as what I *wasn't*. I'm not a novelist. I'm not a wife, or a mother, or a girlfriend. I'm not even a writer anymore. And I haven't been for a long time." Her voice drops to a barely audible whisper. "Nothing has made any sense without Lizzie in the world." She presses her hands against her chest. "And then I thought, I'm not even a sister anymore. It was like losing her changed everything about me that mattered. All the things that I was that added value to the world were gone, and I am nothing." She drags in a tortured breath. "I had this burning desire to see Mom and Dad, but not just to visit them for a few days. I looked up my lease and it was up in five weeks. It felt like a sign. I sold off all my furniture to pay my last month's rent and shipped a dozen boxes to Mom and Dad's, and then I got in my car. Somehow, in my brain, it seemed like this big, trepidatious step toward reclaiming—" She shakes her head. "I don't even know what."

"And then you got here and they weren't home."

Her huge golden-brown eyes meet mine and she blinks. And blinks again. "I didn't know what to do when my first grand plan just to do something. . . didn't work."

So she drove here, the only other place with a connection to Elizabeth, and she heard Amy calling Mary 'Mom.' It finally makes sense. Maybe Mary's right. People who are being awful are usually hurting badly themselves. "I wasn't kidding when I said you're welcome here."

Anica's smile is nearly identical to Elizabeth's. But instead of gutting me like it would have a few years ago, the similarity warms my heart. It feels like Elizabeth's still with me, her effervescent joy warming the entire room. "Thanks."

Perhaps Anica feels like she's the one letting her sister down, not me. It wouldn't be the first time someone projected their own insecurities onto innocent bystanders. I'd like to help her if I can, but I have other priorities that come first. I hop to my feet. "Alright."

She looks up at me. "Alright, what?"

"Your sister would be the first one to chastise you for

mistreating the woman who is bringing joy back to her family."

Her mouth drops open.

"You have been miserable since she died, and believe me when I say that I understand that. You have no idea how well I understand. But you don't love Elizabeth more than I do because you're still suffering. The degree to which you wallow is not an indication of the depth of your pain."

"You've replaced her already." Her mouth hardens. "Pardon me if I question the depth of your suffering."

"She'd want you to find joy too."

"I can't replace a sister," she says.

"I don't think replace is the right word, and I'm not sure your assumption that you can't find someone to take the position she held in your life is true either," I say. "But I know this for an absolute fact. Being happy is a choice, and it's one your sister would want you to make. You really are welcome here, but if I hear that you're making Mary unhappy, I'll toss you out myself. Your sister would never forgive me if I didn't."

Anica doesn't respond, and I hope it means she's processing my words.

Either way, when I hear the grinding of the garage door opener, it's time for me to check on my wife and daughter —and our new pet.

Lucy the chicken lady is just leaving, and Amy waves goodbye briefly and then hunches over the chicken box, stroking Hope's back.

"So what's the verdict?"

"Well, the first injection has been administered," Mary says. "And tomorrow morning, I'll give her the second. But for now, all we can really do is wait and see whether it works."

"And hope," Amy says.

"Which is why that name you chose is brilliant," I say.

"Lucy said I wasted my time picking out those maggots," Amy says.

Huh?

Mary cough-laughs. "Lucy explained that maggots only eat dead flesh, so they might have actually been helping as long as they didn't spread the infection, which likely came from Andy's mouth in any case."

"You're saying I didn't wash the wound well enough?" I pretend to be offended, but I'll gladly shoulder the responsibility for it if Amy feels better as a result. I'd do most anything to spare her guilt.

My darling wife rolls her eyes with forced playfulness. "You Mannings are all desperate to take the blame, aren't you?"

"You're no better," I say.

Mary brushes her fingers across the top of Amy's head. "I know you're worried, but it's time for bed, little one. Just as Hope needs her rest, so do you."

"Can you show me tomorrow?" She looks up at Mary, pleading with her eyes. "Can you show me how to feed her?"

"It's hard, Amy. You have to hold the food and the chicken just so."

"I can do it." Her lip juts out and I wish Anica was in here watching the interchange. Amy's polite resolve is classic Elizabeth, and I can finally enjoy the echoes of it without being pained by the memories.

"Sure," Mary says. "Yes, I'll let you help me tomorrow after school." She's exhausted and I want to do something about it, but I'm not quite sure what to do.

After Amy's asleep, Mary finally takes a bath and climbs into bed herself.

"You alright?"

Mary covers her face with a hand. "It's been a very long day." She explains about her ultimatum to Peter.

"Bravo," I say. "Finally."

"I get it," she says doggedly. "Why he wants to protect him, I mean. I would never be able to fire Amy."

I shake my head. "You would."

Her eyes widen like I slapped her. "How can you say that?"

She bristles when I wrap my arms around her, but I ignore it. "You love her enough to do what's best for her. When your kid messes up, you need to tell them. Your job is to teach them how to make things right. You'd do that for Amy because you care more about her than you do about avoiding uncomfortable situations. Your boss is a coward. You did the right thing today."

"What if I lose my job?"

I laugh. "You're the only one who would be sad about that."

"I'm not the kind of woman to sit around the house and arrange flowers or clip coupons." Her voice could cut glass.

"Don't I know it." I chuckle. "Mary, if you lose your job, it was for all the right reasons, and you'll call any of the other accounting firms in town and get a new one immediately. Or you'll start your own firm, and LitUp will be your first client."

"But—"

I press one finger to her mouth. "You're the best thing that ever happened to Frank & Meacham, and they're smart enough to realize that. Don't worry."

"Okay."

"Besides. A few weeks off when you're about to have a new baby wouldn't be a terrible thing."

"I guess not." She leans back against me, and I know I'm forgiven.

"So what are we thinking about this chicken business?"

Mary's laugh is half cry. "I spent over a hundred dollars on chicken junk at the feed store, and I doubt she'll survive the night."

"Maybe we named her wrong," I say.

"What?"

"We should have named her Million Dollar Chicky."

She slaps at my arm. "Stop."

"But seriously, what does Lucy think?"

"I wish she knew. I feel sick knowing that I might have circumvented this whole mess by simply putting my foot down when Amy asked to bring it home."

"That's not who you are, and it's not who you want Amy to be either. You fight for things, always, even when it's something small, like a chicken. You do it even when you're already exhausted, and I love that. But please tell me you aren't going to work at four a.m. tomorrow."

Mary's nostrils flare. "I finished my reports, and my official maternity leave starts next week anyway. It would serve them right if I didn't go in at all."

"But you will."

"I will."

I groan, but I set my clock for three-forty-five a.m. without mentioning it to my lovely wife. Because if that chicken isn't doing better, I'll be darned if Mary's going to face it alone or be stuck disposing of its body. I'll do that myself.

5

AMY

Dad made fun of me last Christmas when I asked for Santa to bring me a clock that would wake me up. But I know Mary gets up really, really early, and if Hope. . .

I don't want to wake up and find out that she's just gone. So after Mary puts me to bed, I set my alarm for really, really early. I've never gotten up at five in the morning before, but that has to be earlier than Mary leaves because Mattie at school says it's still dark at five in the morning. I never wake up until seven, but I figure she's probably right.

The next morning, when a loud beeping sound wakes me up, I almost turn off my alarm and go back to sleep. But then I remember why I turned it on last night.

Hope!

I jump out of bed and run down the hall toward the garage.

The kitchen lights are already on.

Is that bad? Maybe Dad leaves them on all night. Or does it mean that I'm too late? My hands shake as they turn the doorknob that opens the door into the garage.

That light is on, too. I expect Mary, but it's not Mary sitting on a stool next to Hope's box.

It's Dad. And he's murmuring something.

"Uh, hey."

He yanks his hand out of the box, and when he looks at me, his face looks weird. Like when I caught him actually laughing at a joke while watching *Dinosaur Train* with Chase. "Kiddo, what are you doing up so early?"

"Is Hope alive?"

His smile is the best thing I've seen. "She is. She actually looks much better."

"Is she eating?"

He shakes his head. "Not on her own, but Mary showed me how to feed her. She said you want to learn."

"I do." I walk over to the box.

"It's a little tricky." He snorts. "Or maybe a lot tricky. And it's frustrating. And also pretty messy."

I look at the smears on his pants. One is kind of brownish and one is white. Maybe that one's yogurt. "I don't care," I say. "I want to help."

"Well, I just dosed her with her aspirin water, right after Mary fed her. But if we don't overdo it, we can feed her again before you go to school."

"Good."

"You should go back to sleep."

I put one hand on my hip. "Why aren't you sleeping? It's dark outside." Mattie was totally right.

Dad glances down at the box. "I didn't get it before, you know. Not at all."

"Huh?"

"When you and Mary came back with this half dead bag of feathers and told me we were going to put her in a box in our garage, I was confused."

"Oh." I squat down next to the box and pet Hope's

head. She closes her eyes like she likes it, and she's sitting up again. Dad's right—she looks way better.

"After helping care for her today, I think maybe I do. It's comforting somehow, doing something for a critter that can't care for itself. She's sweet and she's in trouble, and even if it's messy, taking care of her is oddly rewarding."

"You like her." I smile.

"I do." Dad strokes her wing. "Much more than I expected to."

"Oh good. Then if she lives, can we keep her?"

Dad laughs, and Hope actually jolts a little. Then she fluffs up and settles back down.

"Is that a yes?"

"It's a maybe."

"I'll take it," I say.

Dad smacks my leg. "That's because you know that if I say maybe after spending half an hour with her, I'll never kick her out."

"Maybe." It's nice to smile after being afraid all night. I whisper, "You're going to be alright, little girl."

"Let's not get ahead of ourselves, Amy."

"Why?" I scrunch my nose. "Why do people say that? Isn't it good to get ahead?"

He groans as he stands up. "You ask too many questions."

"You only get crabby when you don't know the answer."

He picks me up under the armpits and spins me around. "And you're too smart for your own good. Now go wash your hands and go back to sleep. I'll wake you up in an hour so you can try and feed this mite-bitten bag of feathers." He puts me down.

"What are mites?"

"Tiny bugs that live on birds underneath their feathers," Dad says. "It's like lice for birds—but I would strongly recommend you avoid googling it. Some of the images online are downright horrifying." He shudders.

"Hope doesn't have mites." Or at least, I hope she doesn't. "Right?"

He laughs. "No. Now go to bed."

I can't sleep, of course. So when Dad comes to my room in an hour, I'm dressed and my teeth are brushed. "I'm ready."

"You didn't go back to sleep, did you?"

I shrug like Mary does sometimes when he already knows the answer, and then I walk past him.

Feeding Hope is hard. And it's messy. And I get frustrated. But I do manage to get a few bites of pellets and a little yogurt down her throat. Dad makes her drink a little and we call it good.

"I'll get better," I say.

"I believe you."

"Okay."

To show Dad that I appreciate him, I make Chase's lunch and mine. "I even put fruit in there." I smile. "A banana." They're always all nasty and brown at lunchtime, but Mary makes us take a fruit and a vegetable in each lunch.

"What about the veggie?" Dad lifts one eyebrow.

"I put carrots in mine."

He checks anyway. "Three carrots? That's it?"

"That's how many we have to eat at dinner."

He laughs. "Oh fine."

On the way to school, something occurs to me. "Hey you're going to work today, right?"

Dad grunts, which I think means yes.

"So, who's going to feed Hope?"

"I hadn't thought about it."

Oh, no.

"I bet your Aunt Anica can do it."

"Dad!"

"What?"

"She doesn't care about the chicken, and it's hard to feed her and no one has showed her how. Or how much."

"Mary's going to be home early today, so even if Anica doesn't help, it'll be fine." Dad stops at a light and turns around. "Have you ever known Mary to be irresponsible or forget to line things up?"

I slowly shake my head.

"This is no different. She said she would help Hope, so she'll take care of it."

He's right. Mary always does everything right. Everything.

Like she told me she'd take care of me. Even if she doesn't want to after the new baby comes, she will. But will she still want to? I wish I knew. I hate Piper for making me think about it. I sit as far away from her as I can all day, but at lunch she slides onto the bench across from me while Lacy and Mia take the seats on either side of her. "What's up, loser?" she asks with a smile. Like she's kidding.

Which I know she's not.

I ignore her.

She's wearing a hot pink shirt with a sequin star on it that says DIVA in large letters, so she's hard to ignore. But I do it. I look down so much that I notice her shoes are also covered with bright silver sequins.

No matter what Mary said, she doesn't look much like she's suffering.

"Three carrots?" Piper laughs. "Wouldn't you be sad if all you could afford was three carrots a day, Mia?"

"I can afford as many as I want," I say.

"Sure you can, Mrs. Hannigan." Piper crosses her arms.

It's hard to keep my mouth shut, but every time I open it, she just makes me feel dumber. So I eat my three carrots and my mushy banana and I stare at the ground. But part of me wishes I'd taken the role of Annie, just so she couldn't have it.

Because the look on her face when she found out I took her spot would have been awesome.

Finally lunch is over, and it's time to go to the playground. I usually sit on the swings by myself, and I like swinging alone so it's fine. Actually, it's usually the best part of my day. I stand up, my lunchbox in one hand.

"Hey what's on your pants?" Mia asks.

When I look down, I realize that somehow, even though I fed Hope in my pajamas, I got some of her mashed pellets on my jeans. I gulp. I know it's chicken feed, but it looks kind of like. . .

"Maybe she can't afford to wash her clothes either," Lacy says.

"Is it poop?" Piper asks. "Because it looks like poop."

I clamp my mouth closed. Nothing I say will make this better. When the line finally moves and I can go outside, I burst onto the playground and run toward the swings. Feeling like I can fly always helps.

But not today.

Today I can't even bring myself to push back and forth on the swings. Today I sit and kick at the dirt clumps on the ground, all crackly and weird. And all alone. I'm like a dirt clump and everyone else in school with me is like the grass. I look over at the grass—all green and happy. No wonder they don't want to be my friend. I'm just a dirt clump.

I kick at the dirt underneath my feet until the toes of my sneakers are brown and the dirt clumps are all broken up.

My next class is choir and singing all the songs from Annie in choir is fun. Since I stand in the corner, no one picks on me. That's nice, too.

By the time school ends and it's time for play practice, I

wish I wasn't doing the play at all. I really do *not* want to spend the next two hours with Piper. I'm biting my lip when I walk into to gym.

Coach Brian is looking at something on a clipboard, but when I walk through the door he looks up. "Amy." He beams. "How are you today?"

Something about his smile makes me feel better. "I'm okay."

"Well, maybe by the end of practice today, you'll be great."

"Maybe."

"Have you looked at your lines yet?"

I shake my head, feeling bad again. "Sorry."

"That's fine. It's only the first practice. We'll see how you do, and then you can start working on learning the ones that need the most work first."

"Okay."

"Are you nervous about remembering all the words?"

I have a good memory. Mary says it's like a steel trap. I think that means that it's really hard and moves fast, maybe. "Not really."

"Great." He hands me a stack of paper stapled at the top. "Here's your official copy of the play, in case you lost the one we passed out for tryouts."

I didn't, but I forgot it at home. "Thanks."

Other kids start to walk through the door, and I turn to find a chair. "Do you mind if I ask why you wanted the part you chose?" Coach Brian's eyes are light, light blue, and he's only curious. He doesn't look angry or annoyed. Actually, for an old man, he has a nice smile. And his arms have big muscles in them.

"Hey did you used to play some kind of sports? Like basketball?" I think I heard that from some of the moms once.

He frowns. "What?"

"Someone said you made a lot of money doing some sport and you—" Uh oh. They said he cracked up and that's why he's here. But I forgot that part until just right now.

He drops into a seat and pats the one next to him. "Sit."

"Okay."

"How about this?" he whispers. "If you tell me why you wanted the part of Mrs. Hannigan, I'll tell you whether or not I used to play a sport."

"Okay." It feels like he's being serious, and I think maybe this is something he doesn't want to share, like I don't want to answer his question. It seems like a fair trade. "Piper wanted to be Annie," I whisper. "And I didn't. . ."

Coach's eyes widen. "You didn't want to make her mad, and you thought she might not be upset if you played the bad guy."

I shrug. "Maybe."

"That might have been the most honest thing I've heard all day." He sighs. "I guess that means I have to tell you something I haven't talked to anyone about in a long time."

"I thought everyone would ask you," I say without thinking. Then I clap my hand over my mouth.

Coach Brian's smile is big. "A lot of people have asked me, but I haven't answered."

I wouldn't want to talk about it if I cracked up, either. "But you're going to tell me, right?"

"I am, because you're the first person who has asked about what I did before I came here because you *care* about knowing the answer, instead of trying to pry."

Why else would someone ask something? What does pry mean? I want to ask, but I worry that if I do, he'll answer that instead of the question I want to know more. But that makes me feel bad for asking it at all. "You don't have to tell me if you don't want to."

Coach Brian smiles. "It's fine. Look, I was a baseball

player. A catcher, actually, for a team here in town called the Atlanta Braves. But one day not so long ago, my mom died suddenly." His hands grip the clipboard really hard.

"I'm sorry."

"She was a teacher," he says. "My mom was, I mean. She taught kindergarten for more than twenty years." He meets my eye. "And I don't know how to explain it, really. She made less money in that twenty years than I had made in a single year, but she had also helped more people in one year than I had ever helped. So, that afternoon, instead of negotiating my new contract, I told my agent I'd be retiring when mine was up."

"And you became a teacher."

He laughs. "Does that sound dumb?"

"Not to me," I say. "You're way better than the coach we had last year. And I'm really excited to do a play, which they never had enough volunteers to do for the second graders before."

"My mom directed plays, and when I was a kid, she was the director for my play every year. I don't have any kids, so I figured I'd do a play for the grade that never gets one."

"Well, thanks," I say.

For the rest of practice, when I'm not in a scene, I think about what he said. Coach Brian seems like someone who cares more about other people than he does about himself. And I'm not sure, but he and Lucy look like they might be the same age.

After our last song, Mrs. Tassain claps her hands. "Amy! That was wonderful. Carol Burnett herself couldn't have found fault with it."

Who?

But Piper realizes it's a compliment, even if she doesn't know the lady either, I can tell she's ticked. On our walk toward the front of the school to be picked up, she and Lacy and Mia beeline toward me.

"Bet you're pretty proud of yourself," Piper says. "But—"

"She should be proud," Coach Brian says.

He noticed them coming after me.

Piper's mouth dangles open in a very satisfying way. "Right. I mean, she should be, yeah."

"You should spend a little more time practicing and a little less time opining on the merits of other students," Coach Brian says.

Piper and Mia and Lacy trot a few feet away and whisper and giggle. I hear the words *loser* and *baseball* and *fired*.

"Does it bother you that people talk about you?" I ask.

"Sometimes," he says.

"I'm sorry I asked you about the sports thing."

Coach Brian shakes his head. "You did nothing wrong. I think you'll learn that some people can't find their way toward the light, even when it's all around them, while other people bring light into every room with them. You keep being one of those people, alright? You're the reason I decided to teach, not the Pipers of the world."

An idea occurs to me. A weird idea. An idea that probably won't work. But once it does, I can't stop thinking about it. "Did you know that I have a chicken at my house?" I ask.

"Excuse me?" Coach Brian asks.

"My dog accidentally almost killed a chicken."

"What?" He looks distressed.

"But don't worry. Great Pyrenees are actually really nice. They don't usually attack chickens, and we're taking care of the chicken who got hurt. I named her Hope."

"Oh." The lines around his eyes and mouth go away. "Well, that's neat."

"Do you like chickens?"

Coach Brian shrugs. "Sure. I mean, I like eggs. I like to eat them."

I cringe.

"But I mean, I don't *have* to eat them—not the pets I mean." He frowns. "This sounds bad. What I mean is, yes, I like chickens."

"Then maybe you would want to come visit her sometime."

"Uh," Coach Brian says. "Well."

"It would mean a lot to me." Maybe I'm pushing too hard.

"Well, if your mom says it's okay, sure. Maybe sometime."

"Okay, great!"

Mary's waiting for me outside, her white car parked on the edge of the sidewalk. Chase waves really big when he sees me. Somehow, between that and Coach Brian's words, I don't care about Piper being mean. Because I have a lot of light around me.

"Hey sweetheart," Mary says. "How was your day?"

I sling my backpack into the backseat. "Pretty good, actually."

Mary beams. "Great news."

"I'm a really horrible Mrs. Hannigan."

The smile disappears. "Uh oh. What do you—"

"No," I interrupt. "I mean, she's a bad person, so I'm supposed to be awful, and I'm good at it."

"Oh, well, good then."

"How's Hope?"

"She's good," Chase says. "But she keeps making it hard for Mom to feed her. She's a butthead."

"What?" I ask.

"She was struggling against me more on the last feeding than she has before," Mary says. "And I might have called her a name or two when I spilled yogurt all over, but I think it's a good sign. After all, chickens who are about to die don't have the energy to struggle, right?"

"I fed her today."

"Your dad told me. You can help me feed her tonight, before dinner." She pulls out onto the road, headed for home.

As we drive past, I notice that Piper's still standing on the curb. Her mom's not at the school yet. I hope she has to wait all night, but then I feel guilty for wishing that. "Did Dad tell you I asked if we can keep Hope?"

Mary sighs. "He did mention it, but she has friends back at Lucy's house. I'm not sure that's such a great plan."

"We could get her some new friends," I say. "They have chicks at the feed store since it's springtime. Lucy said so."

"She did," Mary says. "And we can definitely talk about it."

Which is almost the same as no.

I fold my arms across my chest, leaning against the seatbelt. Of course Mary doesn't want to keep Hope or get chicks. She has a new baby coming, my new little brother. I should be happy, probably. I should understand that babies are a lot of work. Dad's told me often enough.

But I love Hope, and I want to keep her.

"If we did get a few chicks, we'd need to get a chicken coop too," Mary says. "And they're a lot of work. With the baby—"

"I know," I say. "You won't have time."

"I was going to say that I'd need a lot of help with any extra pets if we did decide to do that."

"Oh." I think about it. "I can help. A lot."

I can almost hear the smile in her voice. "Maybe you can."

"I want chicks," Chase says. "They're so cute."

"When have you seen chicks?" Mary asks.

"At the farm field trip last year," he says. "Dewberry Farms. They had them. They're so fluffy."

"See? You might love the chicks," I say.

"I might," Mary says. "They would probably be easier to care for than Hope." She laughs. "At least they'd feed themselves."

She might like baby chicks better than Hope, a chicken who's broken and needs a lot of help. Just like she might like the new baby more than me. The baby won't cause problems at school. The baby isn't such a loser that the other kids pick on him. And the baby is actually hers.

Suddenly I don't really want new chicks. I just want to keep Hope and have that be enough.

But probably it's already too late for that.

6

AMY

The next week goes by super-duper fast. I learn all my lines, and I learn to feed Hope on my own. I'm actually better than Mary at feeding her yogurt, anyway. Hope perks up when she sees me, but that may be because Mary gives her shots and I never do. Either way, she still won't eat or drink on her own, but she's still alive and sometimes she even stands up.

I've start taking her outside for an hour after dinner each night while I work on my lines. She mostly just scootches up next to me, but she looks around at the sky and the leaves and the grass, and I think it makes her feel better.

"Lucy's coming over later," Mary announces on Tuesday during dinner.

"What?" I ask.

"She wants to check on Hope's back."

"Oh no," I say. "Tonight won't work. Aunt Anica said she has a headache."

Mary frowns. "Why would you want to—"

"Can you change it?"

"Why?"

"I think Hope's too tired today to get poked and shifted and—"

"What's going on?" Mary drops her napkin on the table.

I can't think of anything that will make sense. Other than the truth. Crap. "Um, I had an idea. You might think it's weird."

Dad frowns. "What kind of idea?"

"She's trying to explain, if you two would stop interrupting," Aunt Anica says.

"I think tonight is too busy," I say. "And I don't want Aunt Anica's headache to get worse with more people."

Mary laughs. "Lucy won't even come inside the house. She's coming to see the chicken in the garage."

"It's just that I think tomorrow will be better," I say. "I asked Coach Brian to come tomorrow."

"Wait," Luke says. "Coach Brian of the dreamy eyes and bulging muscles? The retired basketball star, Coach Brian?" He pins me with a stare.

My cheeks are hot. "No, he played baseball."

"Why, pray tell," Dad asks, "do you want him to come over?"

"He's, well, he's a s-s-super nice guy," I stammer.

"Okay." Mary smiles. "And?"

"If you think I need a setup," Anica says, "then—"

I laugh. Then I laugh some more. "Not you. Coach Brian is super *nice*."

"Lucy." Mary's smile is so big it makes me smile back. "You want Coach Brian to meet Lucy."

"Yes, Lucy. She said she wanted a guy who cares more about others. Did you know he quit baseball so he could teach? Because his mom taught and he wanted to help kids like she did."

"So he's good looking, possibly a saint, and you *don't*

want to set him up with me because he's nice?" Aunt Anica looks irritated.

"You just got all mad," I say. "When you thought—"

"Women aren't safe," Dad whispers. "Don't expect her to make sense."

Anica throws a pea at him.

"Hey, no throwing food," Chase says. "Mom says."

"Right," I say. "But about Lucy?" I try to make pleading eyes like Chase does at Mary. "Maybe she can come tomorrow. And you can tell Coach Brian after practice that it's fine if he comes over to meet Hope."

Dad spears a piece of chicken with his fork. "There's no way he will want to—"

"He already told me he will." Kind of. "If Mary says it's okay."

"Well, if you've already set this up," Mary says. "Far be it for me to get in the way." She whips out her phone and starts tapping. "Lucy says tomorrow is alright. I told her right at five-fifteen."

"Perfect," I say.

I'm eating my last bite of chicken when the doorbell rings. Chase is faster than me, usually, but this time I beat him to the door. For some reason, I thought maybe it was Lucy anyway. I wanted to try and get some more information about what kind of person she likes. Or maybe I could say something about Coach Brian to make her think about him.

But it's not Lucy. It's just Aunt Trudy, and she's already getting married so she doesn't need my help.

"Hey Aunt Trudy," I say, freezing mid-hug. Would Mom not want me to call her Aunt, either? Will Aunt Anica get mad that I did? I turn around slowly to see if anyone else heard me.

But I'm the only one who left the kitchen. Probably because Mary knows it's Aunt Trudy.

"Hey, is it a bad time?" Aunt Trudy asks.

I shake my head. "No, we're just finishing dinner. It's fine." I point. "Your sister's in there."

"My sister?" Aunt Trudy looks. . . I don't know what to call it. Like I said something funny.

"Mary."

"I know her name, munchkin."

"Where's Troy?" I look around.

"He's with Uncle Paul," she says. "I actually came by to talk to you."

Mary walks into the family room. "Is it Trudy?" She smiles when she sees her sister. "Hey."

"I was just telling Amy here that I need to talk to her."

"Ah, right." Mary bobs her head. "Well, I'll leave you to it."

I don't understand. "You came all the way over here to talk to me?"

She nods slowly, like this is a big deal. Did I do something wrong? Did Mary tell her I'm not calling her 'Mom'? Is she mad?

"Hey, it's not a job interview," Aunt Trudy says. "Calm down." She points at the sofa in the living room. "Can we sit for a second?"

I gulp.

She beams and shakes my shoulder a little. "Seriously. I need to talk to you about something good."

Good? I follow her over and sit down. "What?"

"You know I'm getting married in a few days."

"Yeah."

"Well, there's this thing I need."

"Oh!"

"Would you be willing to be a flower girl for me?"

I beam.

"It's a big job. I can't ask Chase and Troy. They'll chuck

handfuls of flower petals at guests. You'll need to toss them carefully, and scatter them evenly."

Another idea occurs to me. "People dress up for weddings, right?"

Trudy frowns. "Yes."

"And people dance and stuff? And they talk about love and getting married?"

She nods. "I don't understand—"

I tell her about Lucy and Coach Brian, and how I'm going to try and get them to meet tomorrow.

"That's a cute idea," she says. "But I don't see—"

"Maybe Hope can be another flower girl. Don't you usually have two?"

"Who's Hope?" Aunt Trudy asks, looking around.

I laugh. "It's my chicken. Weren't you listening? That's how I know Lucy."

"Ah," she says. "But a chicken can't be a flower girl."

"It's not like you *really* need her to be a flower girl." I sigh. For an adult, Aunt Trudy isn't being that smart. "She's just the excuse. So I can invite Lucy to help with her during the wedding. Then she'll need a date, and I can suggest she take someone who happens to be right there in my garage too." I tilt my head. "Coach Brian."

Aunt Trudy shakes her head like Andy does sometimes, like she's trying to shake something off. "Whoa. You are a *lot* like your mom."

I frown. "You didn't even know my mom."

"I meant Mary," Aunt Trudy says. "You're a lot like Mary." But she looks hurt. Like I said something bad.

"Oh."

"She was the smartest little girl I'd ever seen, maybe until right now."

"Oh." I swallow. "Thanks, I guess."

Aunt Trudy lowers her head a little. "I could not

possibly pay you a higher compliment, you know. I don't know anyone smarter than my big sister. Or anyone kinder. Or anyone with more love in her heart. So to say you remind me of her with this bizarre setup, well, it's a huge compliment."

"So will you help?"

Aunt Trudy eyes me for a moment. "Sure. But let's think this through. A chicken can't possibly toss flowers. But maybe she could be the ring bearer." Her eyes practically twinkle. "And I suppose the guests will survive if a few handfuls of petals pelt them in the face."

"What?"

"I think this will only work if you say that you and Hope will be my ring bearers, and the boys will be my flower—er." She clears her throat. "My flower guys."

"Does this ruin your wedding?" I scrunch my nose.

Aunt Trudy wraps an arm around my shoulders. "What do you think weddings are about, kiddo?"

I shrug.

"This is my second one, because it took me a while to get this right. Maybe you can learn from my mistakes. Weddings are about love and family, and I can't think of a better way to honor both than to support my favorite niece in her plans to bring love to two people who have no idea what's barreling their way."

I look down at my feet. "Well, I better go check on Hope."

"You do that." Aunt Trudy drops a kiss on my head.

I rush out of the room, hoping she didn't notice that I'm crying.

The next day, I corner Coach Brian before practice. "Hey Coach."

"Oh, hey, Amy. I meant to tell you, the way you have memorized those lines is an inspiration."

Ooh, this could be a good way to work Hope into the

conversation. "Thanks. I sit outside with my recovering pet chicken every day and work on them."

The side of his mouth turns up in a weird half smile. "Well, that's an interesting method I've never heard of, but if it works for you, great. Maybe you should try and memorize Annie's lines too, just in case."

"In case what?" What's he talking about?

"You never know what might happen." He shrugs. "What if Piper got sick? Who would step in? If you knew the lines, we could make Laura take over for you, maybe. And we could still have the play."

I frown. "I already know all of Annie's lines." I clear my throat. "I'm not an orphan. My mother and father left a note saying they loved me and they were coming back for me." I toss my hair.

Coach Brian laughs. "Brilliant."

I roll my eyes. "I just wanted to tell you something before practice starts."

"Oh?"

"Hope is doing so well that my mom said it's fine!"

"Huh?"

"I asked her if you can come meet Hope, and she said yes, but that you needed to come today. Because my Aunt is getting married soon and things are really busy. So can you?"

"Can I?" He blinks. "Can I come see your chicken?"

"Yes." I keep my eye on him. People try and change their mind sometimes unless you really stare at them.

"Uh well, I guess so. But I can't stay for more than a minute."

I can't keep from smiling. "Great. A minute is fine. I mean, it's only a chicken. How long will it take?" I spin around on my heel and run to a seat. It's hard to pay attention to the practice when I'm so excited.

At the end, Mrs. Tassain hands me a bag. "This is your costume. I need you to try it on and make sure it will fit."

"Oh," I say. "Okay, thanks."

Coach Brian is disappearing out the door, so I sprint to catch up. "Hey, Coach."

"Oh. Hi, Amy. I was looking for you."

It didn't look like it. I was right in front of him when he left. "Well, I'm here. Are you ready? Maybe you can follow us—"

"I'm not sure—"

I shake my head. "It won't take long. Please?"

"Alright." He sighs. "You're a persistent little thing. I'll give you that."

But he's coming. That's what matters.

"Hey," I say when I hop in the car.

"Is everything a go?" Mary glances back at me.

I smile. "It is."

"Great." She waves at Coach Brian. "You want to follow me?"

Mrs. Tassain taps on the window and Mary rolls it down. "I hear Coach Brian has an invite to see this royal chicken Amy is always talking about. Mine must have gotten lost in the mail."

My mouth drops open.

"You wouldn't be trying to set him up, would you?" Mrs. Tassain whispers.

Mary laughs, like a full out, belly laugh.

"I'll take that as a yes, and in that case, I'm happy to stand here with the kids alone while he ditches me to go to Casa Manning." Mrs. Tassain throws me a thumbs up. "Good luck."

Huh. People are pretty nice, if you give them the chance to be. I notice Piper—her mom must be late again—scowling at me as we drive away.

Some people, anyway.

"I hope you had a great day," Mary says.

"I did," Chase says. "I made a fossil today."

"You *made* a fossil?" I ask.

"With salt bread." He beams. "Wanna see?"

A crusty, flat piece of bread with a tiny dinosaur skeleton, probably from a toy, is pressed into my face. "That's great," I say. "Really cool."

"It is." Chase snatches it back and pokes at it.

That won't survive the day. "I had a good day too."

"Good," Mary says. "Because I need to ask you about something."

"You do?" For some reason that makes me nervous. "Is Aunt Anica alright?"

Mary groans. "By 'alright' do you mean, is she still lounging around the house all the time in her pajamas, grumbling?"

"I guess so."

"Then she's fine."

"Okay."

"But Geo called me today."

"Your friend Geo?"

Mary nods. "Her business is doing so well that she needs to hire a new employee. There's a lady she liked, but she was nervous about her."

"Why are you telling me?" I ask.

"Well, it turns out the woman's daughter goes to school with you." Mary stops at the same stop light where we always get stuck. "Geo thought you might have some insight into what kind of employee she would be, based on what kind of parent she is."

Uh-oh. "Who is it?" But I already know. She would have just asked if I knew her if it was anyone else. Mary knows that I know one person in particular.

"It's Piper."

Of course it is. I groan. "What did you tell her?"

"I told her that Piper was a little jerk," Mary says. "I told her she made your life miserable and that it was almost certain that her mother was awful too. I said that if she hired her, I'd never talk to her again."

My heart soars. "You did?"

"I did."

I can't stop my smile.

"But then, I thought about my daughter."

Her daughter. It makes me happy and sad at the same time. Am I her daughter? And if I am, am I still my real mom's daughter? Why is this so confusing?

"And I thought about the kind heart my daughter has."

What does that mean, a kind heart? Does it mean that I shouldn't want something bad to happen to Piper, the girl who's always so mean to me? Because I do, and I feel kind of embarrassed about that. "What if I don't have a kind heart?"

Mary shrugs. "That would be okay. But I told you before that I suspected Piper might be having trouble. What kind of person do you think looks for a new job?"

I gulp.

"Did you know that I lost my job on Monday?" Mary's words are tight, like they hurt to say. "It was the right decision, and I don't regret it. But it still hurts. I loved my job, and I worked hard at it, and to not have a job I love, well. Even though your dad makes plenty of money and we don't need the money I make to pay our bills, losing it was hard for me. If I *did* need the money from my job to pay my bills, like I needed it before I met your dad, well." She sighs. "That would be even harder. I might be mean or crabby or rude."

"I guess." I don't really pay a lot of attention to other people, usually. But Piper is always waiting for her mom.

"Piper's mother was working as a store clerk at the grocery store. She has been wanting to plan events, but she hasn't ever done it. Geo wanted to know how she dealt with people when she wasn't interviewing for a job. When I told her how her daughter treated you, she said she'd never hire her."

That makes me feel really bad.

"And then I felt guilty about what I said, about maybe making someone whose life is hard even harder." Mary's quiet after that.

Chase sings a song about a tooty-tot.

"Maybe—" But I can't quite say it. I'm not nearly as nice as Mary thinks I am.

"Maybe what?" The hope in her voice hurts.

"Maybe Piper's mean because you pick me up on time every day and her mom's always late." I bite my lip and think about her sequins and sparkly shoes. She can't be that poor. She always has the nicest clothes and shoes. She made fun of me for being poor—she does that a lot. What if. . . "And maybe she'd be nicer if her mom had a job she liked."

"Perhaps," Mary says, "but that's your call. I told Geo that perhaps I was mistaken. I told her I'd talk to you and call her back."

I gulp. Mary told me she wouldn't do anything about the Piper thing, other than offer suggestions, and she did that. She says it's up to me. And I guess I know what Piper would do if she were me, but I don't want to be like her. Even so, it's really, really hard for me to say, "I think. . . I think you should tell Geo to give her mom a chance."

Mary only nods, but when I look at her face in the rear view mirror, she's smiling. It makes me think that I did what she would have done, and that makes me proud.

When we pull into the garage, I nearly forget that Coach Brian is right behind us. I practically leap from the car. "What time is it?"

"Two minutes until Lucy should show up," Mary says with a smirk.

"Oh, I hope this works."

"Are you saying that you hope they'll get married?" Mary's eyes rise quickly. "That is a lot of expectation to put on this little meeting. Maybe we just hope that they'll be friends."

"Lucy's a good person," I whisper. "And so is Coach Brian. I can tell. They should be a lot happier with another good person."

"It's not always quite that simple." Mary laughs. "But I suppose stranger things have happened than a second grader setting up two people successfully."

I throw my bag into the laundry room and race back into the garage. Coach Brian looks pretty uncomfortable talking to Mary, whose stomach is so big it bumps into everything all the time.

"So, this is Hope," I say. "She still has to be force fed every day, every two hours. She won't eat on her own." I sit down by the box. "Here, I can show you how we do it."

Coach Brian's eyebrows rise. "You do it?"

I nod. "It's hard, and sometimes she's kind of annoying to feed, but Mary and Dad let me do it when I'm home."

Coach Brian blinks. "She's very pretty for a chicken. I guess I always thought they were all brown or white. I didn't expect her to be bluish grey. Or for her feathers to all look so different."

"A lot of them are brown or white," I say. "But she's an Andalusian and they lay white eggs. She can fly too—when she's not hurt."

"Wait, she can?" He crouches down so he's closer to her. She clucks softly.

"I think she likes you," I say.

"How many eggs does she lay?" he asks.

"None right now," a voice behind us says. Lucy! "Who's this?"

Coach Brian leaps to his feet. "Oh." He blinks. "I'm Coach Brian."

"Please tell me you're not a life coach," Lucy says with a funny look on her face.

"I'm a PE coach for Joshua Elementary," he says. "But sometimes it feels like the same thing." He looks down at me. "Stay away from drugs young lady, you hear me?"

It's a dumb joke, but Lucy laughs anyway. I think that's a good sign. "Lucy owns Hope." I frown. "Or she *did* own Hope. She's mine now, right?"

Lucy smiles at me. "She sure is. With the amount of work you guys have been putting in to help her, you've definitely earned the right to keep her as your pet." She crouches over the box. "I came to check on her back."

"What happened?" Coach Brian asks.

"My dog got confused," I say. "But Andy comes with us into the garage all the time now, and she's fine with her. She never even growls or anything. I think she didn't know Hope, and she was worried that since she flew over the fence, she was a threat. Usually Great Pyrenees are really good with chickens. They're guardian dogs."

"Sometimes I think Miss Amy here should be teaching at the school," Coach Brian says. "She might know more than me."

Lucy laughs even harder this time, even though this joke is even worse. I don't know anything about how to teach kids to play baseball or basketball or football. But her laughing makes me smile. "He's the best coach ever," I say. "And he's the director for our musical, too."

"Is he?" Lucy asks. "That kind of makes me feel guilty. I'm not the best at anything."

"I doubt your patients would say that," Mary says. "I'm sure they appreciate your particular skillset a great deal."

"Are you a doctor?" Coach Brian asks.

Lucy shakes her head. "You sound like my mom, but I'll

tell you what I told her. Doctors have to do all the miserable stuff. I'm a nurse. They have to rush from room to room while I have more time to care for each patient. I prefer to nurture the patients, not cut on them."

"Admirable," Coach Brian says. "I've always thought nurses were basically saints."

"Hardly," Lucy says. "But thanks anyway."

"Hey, I needed to ask you for a favor," I say.

"Who?" Coach Brian asks.

"Sorry," I say. "Lucy."

She pokes Hope again and stands up. "Her back is healing up really well. I know it looks scary, but those dragon scales are actually exactly what you want to see at this stage. Her body has covered all the damage—all those holes Andy made with her teeth, and now underneath all that mess, her body is regrowing both skin and muscle. The fact that she can stand now and that she drinks on her own sometimes, well." She shakes her head. "It's practically miraculous, really. I think you're okay to discontinue the antibiotics."

"Coming from a nurse and our chicken expert," Mary says. "That's great news."

"Now if she'll just perk up enough to start eating on her own," Lucy says, "you'll be in the clear." She leans down to pet Hope's head, and then turns to me. "What favor did you want to ask me, little nurse?"

My cheeks heat up. Little nurse. I like that. "Well, my Aunt needs me to be the ring bearer for her wedding this weekend, and she thought it was a good idea if Hope comes with me. She'd be sort of like a symbol of healing and love. My aunt was married to a real jerk before." I smile.

"Okay." Lucy tilts her head. "That's a different idea, but it's kind of cool. I think Hope is calm enough that if you kept her in a box for the wedding, she'd do alright."

"Yeah, that's the favor I wanted to ask. I can't watch

Hope for the whole wedding, and I'd hate it if someone got into her box or if she got scared."

Lucy glances at Mary. "And?"

"So I thought maybe you could come to the wedding, which my aunt says is fine, and kind of keep an eye on Hope. The food is going to be really good, I promise. Aunt Trudy said they'll even have peanut butter and jelly sandwiches if you don't like the weird kinds of food."

"You're sure there will be normal food?" Lucy asks. "Because I really like peanut butter and jelly."

I nod.

"Well, that's a nice thought, but—"

"You don't want to go without a date?" I scrunch my nose. "Yeah, I wondered about that." I tap my lip. "Gosh. I wish I knew another old guy who wasn't married who could go with you. To help make my aunt's dreams for her perfect wedding come true, I mean."

Mary snorts, which does not help. And dumb old Coach Brian doesn't say a word. He stands like a complete dummy, totally quiet. Even singing the tooty-tot song would be more helpful than standing there like that. It's a miracle people get married at all.

"Oh," I say. "Hey, what about you, Coach Brian? Maybe you could be her date?" I beam. "Just so that my aunt and I can have Hope with us."

He still says nothing.

"As the ring bearer," I say, widening my eyes. Get with it, man.

Coach Brian smiles, finally, and says, "Sure. I don't have any other plans. I think I could do that, if Lucy needs a date."

Lucy clears her throat. "I was going to say that I'm working this weekend."

And just like that, I want to cry. I got so close.

"But my friend Shawna owes me a favor. I bet she'd switch shifts with me."

Yes!

"Anything to celebrate true love, right?" Mary asks.

"Right," I say. "Thank you both, so much."

Ha, gotcha.

7

ANICA

I hate when I forget to turn off the ringer on my phone. Although, it's my own fault for picking such an obnoxious ringtone. I finally roll over and answer.

"Hello, is this Miss Anica Maggard?"

I wipe my eyes. Asking for me by my full name is never a good sign. "Uh, yes. Who's this?"

"My name is Katie."

She's way, way too perky for. . .I blink and rub at my eyes until I can make out the bedside clock. Ten-forty. Huh. I guess it's not that early to most people. "Hi Katie. What do you want?"

"Oh, I hope I didn't call at an inconvenient time."

That's a lie. She doesn't care whether it's a bad time for me. Calls are always inconvenient, so I don't bother easing her mind about it. People react oddly to silence.

"Are you still there?"

I grunt.

"Okay, well, I'm currently a student at Princeton."

I groan. It's some idiotic student my alma mater has tasked with trying to pry money out of me. Which is a complete waste of time as, even if I cared to donate to an institution with a twenty-five billion dollar endowment, I have nothing to give. "Well, you've got some bad luck. Because you managed to find probably the only alumnus from your esteemed institution without a penny to her name."

"Oh."

Ha. I've made her feel uncomfortable. Good. Shiny new pennies need to know the feeling every now and then. "And let me give you some free advice while I have you on the phone."

"Um, okay."

"Don't major in English and don't try and write the great American novel, or you might end up just as pathetic as me." I hang up. I try to go back to sleep, but someone's vacuuming outside my door. Even with a pillow over my head, I can't quite drown it out.

I guess it's my own fault. I'm stuck in this house with two little kids and a manic pregnant lady for seven more days until my parents get back. Even when I told them I was in town, they didn't offer me a key. What kind of parents don't let their daughter stay in— Well, if it's not my childhood home since they sold that, at least it's my parents' current home.

Finally, I wake up, take a shower, and brush my teeth. Before I've even finished drying my hair, someone's knocking at the door, probably wondering when she can clean it. "Um, I'll be out in a minute." Although, Luke's cleaning lady might not understand English. "Un minuto," I say. "Muy pronto."

"Excuse me?" Mary's voice is even more annoyed than usual.

I close my eyes. I can't catch a break. "Um, sorry. I heard the vacuum. I thought you might be the cleaning lady."

"I don't have a cleaning lady."

Of course she doesn't. Why would superwoman need a cleaning lady when she's two weeks away from having a baby? "Oh, sorry. I didn't realize that. Is there something I can help you with?"

"I was about to meet Amy for lunch at the school, but it occurred to me that you might want to go."

Sit next to a dozen little munchkins eating ding dongs and Lunchables? Pass. I open my mouth to tell her thanks but no thanks when memories from last night hammer into me. Amy, *laughing* at the idea of setting me up with a hot, formerly professional athlete whom she really likes.

Why was the idea so funny?

Am I really such a big loser that she'd rather set her PE coach up with some wacky chicken lady nurse? Maybe I should go. Maybe I'll meet this coach while I'm there. Then Amy will realize that her Aunt Anica isn't such an embarrassment.

"When would we need to leave?"

"I assumed that if you were going, you'd prefer I stay home," Mary says.

God, she's smug. And I hate that she's always right. "Oh, okay. Well, when do I need to leave, then?"

"Probably in the next twenty minutes. Did you want to go?"

"Sure, yeah. I'll go."

"Wonderful. She'll be so delighted."

Right. Even I know that Amy dramatically prefers her pregnant stepmother to me. Which is another reason why I probably ought to go. I rush to finish my hair and sprint to my room to dress in something presentable. I need an outfit that screams New York Times Bestseller instead of Totally Washed Up Loser. I toss sweaters and dresses over my shoulder into a pile while I rummage through my suitcase.

But then I find it—my blue cashmere sweater. The one

I wore when I went on the Tonight Show. The one that makes me feel like a billion bucks. I tug on some black slacks with it, and I jog out to the kitchen. Mary has drawn a detailed map to get me to the school, a mile away, and then a smaller one of the school with an 'x' over the cafeteria.

"You'll want to take your drivers' license with you," she says, "so the office can print you a name tag."

"Is this a school or a prison?" I ask.

Mary blinks.

"It's a joke, right?" I ask. "Because to most kids, school basically *is* a prison."

She frowns. "They go to an excellent school, and mostly Chase and Amy love it."

"Right," I say. "No, I mean. Okay. Well, I'll see you later, then."

As I walk to my car, I realize it must have been Mary vacuuming and a pang of guilt sideswipes me. I'm loafing around, sleeping all hours, assuming that since Luke is loaded, his wife has an army of people running her house. Meanwhile she's taking care of my niece admirably and cleaning up after both kids and me.

I might really suck.

I'll have to inspect that in a little more depth later, when I'm fortified with more than a bag of stale mini-muffins I find underneath my seat.

Of course Mary's map is to scale and crystal clear, and thanks to the detail, I have zero problems finding the school and then the cafeteria. And I may not have wanted to wake up quite so early or hoof it to an elementary school, but the beaming smile on Amy's face when she sees me, well.

That makes it more than worth it.

I had no idea it would make her so happy to have me

show up for lunch. Geez. That pang of guilt swells up to sucker punch me.

I'm a horrible aunt.

Mary's a pretty decent mother.

And I'm beginning to worry that Lizzie would be heartily ashamed of me.

"Hey, girlfriend," I say enthusiastically.

Amy stands up, abandoning her lunchbox, and races down the aisle between the tiny tables. Her arms wrap around me ridiculously tight. "I'm so glad you came to lunch."

"Of course." And I resolve then and there to come at least once a week while I'm here, however long that is. I bet Chase would like to see me too. "Where should we sit?"

"Oh, you can sit by me." Amy walks toward her My Little Pony lunchbox. "You can have half my sandwich, too. Actually, I'm not that hungry if you want all of it."

"Or you could have one of her carrots," a little girl with shiny, russet hair giggles.

I hate her.

"Who are you?" I sit next to Amy, the kids on either side of her scootching down to make room without being asked, all of them staring at me a little starry-eyed.

"I'm Piper," she says, her head cocked sideways, like I should know what that means.

"So are Amy's carrots really good?" I look to Piper's left and right, my mean-girl senses tingling.

"Well, I hope they are," Piper says with a smug smile.

"Why's that?" I arch my eyebrow for maximum intim-idation.

"She only ever has about three of them," the blonde girl next to Piper says.

"Did it occur to any of you that perhaps Amy isn't a fan of carrots, but her parents send them because they're healthy and they brokered a sophisticated deal that she would eat exactly three—no more, no less?"

Piper's eyes widen.

"I'm guessing you don't bargain with your parents. You look like the kind of kid who gets whatever she wants all the time." I lean forward. "The danger in being a spoiled brat, you see, is that your mother has to put up with you. But as you get older, no one wants to be friends with someone like that."

Her devoted friends laugh just as hard at my joke as they did at her jabs earlier. They're some real winners. Not even loyal.

"My recommendation?"

The three of them look at me, wide-eyed, nervous.

"If I were you, I'd start watching what *Amy* here does. You see, she's perfect at home and at school. And you might find that a little intimidating right now, but when you're older, you'll realize that's the kind of person you want to be. Not the person who makes fun of other people to feel better about themselves."

Piper swallows hard and then stands up. "We'd rather sit somewhere else, thanks."

I smile at her. "I think everyone here would appreciate that. We're all tired of the smell, frankly."

Every little kid on either side of us has been terrorized by this kid, I realize. Because their laughter is far louder than my somewhat ridiculous taunts warrant.

When I look down at Amy, she's practically hero-worshipping me. Well, at least I've still got my second grade slam-mojo. "That was amazing," Amy says.

"It wasn't," I say. "In fact, I should be apologizing to you right now."

"All Mary does is tell me to be nice to Piper. She says Piper is probably really sad and hurting."

For the love. How is Mary so stinking perfect all the time? I groan inwardly. "She might actually be right," I say.

"But no one has ever told Piper off like that. I think she'll be scared of me now."

Actually, she'll probably come down on poor, sweet Amy even worse once I'm gone. I'm a fifty-pound grenade and she's afraid of me, but I can't be here all the time. I might have sentenced Amy to her doom. "Look, the thing is. . ." How do I get her out of this situation I've now potentially worsened? I'm an idiot.

Amy takes a bite of her sandwich and the movement distracts me.

"What the heck kind of sandwich is that?"

"Oh." Amy scrunches her nose. "It's apple slices, cheese, and mayonnaise."

"That sounds so nasty," I say. "You were offering me half of that?"

Amy shrugs. "Piper's allergic to peanut butter, and I'm not a fan of almond butter or sandwich meat, so me and Mary had to get creative."

Her little voice saying the word 'Mom' on the night I arrived taunts me. She's said 'Mary' ever since that night. I broke things between her and Mary, and I shouldn't have.

I'm like the proverbial bull in Luke's delicately balanced china shop life.

Oh, Lizzie. I'm sorry. I swear I didn't mean to come here and just poop all over everything.

"Wait." Some of the snatches of conversation I've heard over the past ten days start to penetrate and mesh. "Is this the girl who took your part? She's playing Annie?"

Amy gulps. So that's a yes.

"What happens if she eats peanut butter? Because that sandwich she was eating looked a lot like peanut butter."

"She doesn't stop breathing," a little boy next to Amy says. "She just gets a rash. My mom thinks it's dumb that none of us can have peanut butter cause it makes her itchy, but the teachers agreed it's still a good idea."

A thought hatches in my evil brain, but with all these kids listening in on my every word, I can't explain it now. "Well, listen, Amy, I need to clarify something. I know you think it was cool that I set Piper back. But the problem is that she's scared of me, but I don't go to school here."

My poor little niece is wicked smart. Her eyes go round. "You think—"

"Yeah, what I did might have been dumb. She might be worse when I leave."

Amy sets her sandwich down and puts her hands in her lap.

"I'm sorry. If that happens, if I made things worse, I'm really, really sorry. Because Mary was probably right." I drop my voice to a whisper. "If Piper is hurting, if her life is hard or her mom is mean, she's not going to necessarily leave you alone because I scared her off. She might already be used to keeping her head down around the big meanies, and then terrorizing the little guys." Like sweet Amy.

I want to punch Piper in her snooty nose.

"It's fine," Amy says.

"It's fine?"

"If she gets worse, well, it's fine. Because I'll just think about the things you said and how shocked she was, and it'll be easier to ignore her than ever before."

Stupid guilt keeps smacking me over the head harder and harder. Lizzie's daughter is a freaking angel. "Good idea," I say.

When they release the kids to the playground, I ask, "Can I come?"

The tremendous smile that nearly cracks her face in two is enough of an answer for me. There are two sets of swings and for some odd reason she heads straight for the ones at the far end of the playground. Probably because I'm with her, no one else even follows us. We have the entire set of swings to ourselves.

"So kiddo, I had an idea."

"Yeah?" Amy looks almost too eager as she plops into a swing and starts to rock back and forth.

"Your tyrannical overlord is allergic to peanuts, but her reaction's not too bad. A rash, right?"

Amy's face immediately falls. "I guess so."

"What if, on the day of the play, we switch her sandwich out for a peanut butter one? She wouldn't really be in danger, but if she got a rash, she'd probably be out of commission for the play." I smile. That little brat deserves it.

"I'm not sure Gregory really knows what happens to Piper," Amy says. "And—"

I roll my eyes. "But if she's really allergic, she'll have an EpiPen or whatever. They always keep that stuff on hand."

Amy hops off the swing, her hands flying to her hips. "Are you kidding right now? Because I can't tell, but I don't think it's very funny."

"I'm not kidding," I say. "With my help, we could totally pull it off."

"What's wrong with you?" Amy shakes her head. "You may think my real mom would be upset at me for calling Mary 'Mom,' but I'm beginning to think that you don't know anything. Maybe *you* need a new mom if Grandma didn't teach you right from wrong." She huffs and starts walking back to the main playground.

I sink down onto the swing and drop my face in my hands.

Because my darling little niece is right.

I probably need a good paddle on the bum, and losing Lizzie isn't really a good excuse for my behavior, not anymore.

No, at this point, my idiocy is all on me.

❅   8   ❅

LUKE

Paul's backyard looks even better than it did when he hosted my wedding to Mary. I can't help smile, thinking about that day. It was as perfect as any day could be.

Mary wraps one arm around my waist. "What was I thinking, saying yes to Trudy?"

"To holding her wedding ten days before you have a baby?"

"And right at the end of tax season."

"You aren't currently employed." I turn my gorgeous wife's face upward and kiss her. "And I couldn't be more pleased about that."

"Umm, it cost you $200,000. Care to rethink your position?"

"Clarification," I say. "It cost LitUp that amount. Half that loss will be borne by my brother, who wouldn't have even realized there was an error or that we'd overpaid on our taxes if you hadn't insisted on telling him."

She rolls her eyes. "It was my job as your tax preparer to tell you both, and my firm should have made it right."

"But they agreed to buy you out completely, without

any kind of penalty," Luke says. "And that concession resulted in income of what to us?"

"A hundred and thirty thousand dollars." Mary scowls. "Your brother laughed when I offered to pay him a hundred of that to make things right."

"That's good. If he'd taken you up on it, I'd have had to punch his pretty boy face."

Mary swats my arm. "Stop. You'd have done no such thing."

"Paul and I are just glad that we won't have to worry about our taxes ever again, not now that Manning Tax will be handling it."

"I haven't decided whether to start my own firm," Mary says. "And I certainly haven't decided on a name."

I lean close to her ear. "Let's just say that I have ways of being persuasive. I think Manning Tax has an excellent ring to it." I can't help smile when I feel a shiver run up her back. Works every time.

"We're at a wedding, Luke," she says in her school teacher tone.

I love her school teacher tone. "I'm aware. But my brother's big, empty house is *right there* and the ceremony isn't for. . ." I check my watch. "Forty more minutes."

Mary startles. "Forty minutes? I'm supposed to be helping Trudy get ready. Can you check on Amy and Chase and that dumb chicken and make sure they're all fine?"

I think she may love that 'dumb' chicken almost as much as the kids. I smile. "Sure. I'll do that."

I watch fondly as she waddles away, unbelievably cute as a pregnant lady, not that she believes me. I find Chase immediately—squealing at the top of his lungs as Andy completely ignores him and Paul's dumb lab waits to play fetch. Chase and Troy are arguing over who can throw the ball again, but they'll work that out themselves. "Carry on, boys," I say.

They ignore me.

I find Hope not much later, being adequately watched by Lucy and Coach Brian. They may be a little distracted, but I imagine they'll keep a dog or cat from attacking it. I can't help be a little bit proud, as I watch them flirting. Who knew Amy was such a savvy matchmaker? Brian is laughing way too loud at Lucy's jokes, and Lucy can't seem to take her hand off his arm.

But Amy. . .where is she? I figured she'd be watching Lucy and Coach Brian from around the corner. Or playing with the dog. Or petting the chicken. Or ordering the wedding staff around. I can even imagine just how that would go. 'No, that flower arrangement is all wrong.'

I finally duck inside Paul's house, moderately nervous at this point that I still haven't found her.

"I don't care! How can you not understand that? I bought your excuses for the first year, Doug. Over and over, like a moron. But at this point, I just need you to pay the child support. I'm done. If you don't pay me by next Friday when my rent is due, I'm going to file a lien. My lawyer says I can."

Silence.

I creep toward the voice, curious who in the world would be inside his house, yelling at someone right before Paul's wedding.

It's Geo's new wedding planner helper person. And someone's with her—that horrible little brat who's so awful to Amy. Piper's wearing denim shorts, a shirt with a sequin heart, and sparkly sneakers. Certainly not wedding attire. I close my eyes and sigh. Right. Mary mentioned that Geo was going to hire the mother of someone Amy knew. She didn't mention it was *Piper.* I'd have put a stop to that one for sure.

"No, it's not fine if you just—" She growls into the phone. "I'm *working* Doug, at my dream job, not that you care. Today's your weekend so I didn't make other arrangements, and I can't have her here."

She pauses.

"She's not dressed, for one."

A pause.

"I can't afford to buy her a new dress. She wears the same few outfits over and over. How much do you think I made at Kroger?"

Another pause.

"I wouldn't have time to get her one, even if you wanted to pay for it. It's almost time for the ceremony. And she can't stay here. Their little brat hates her for some reason. I guess when your dad is rich as sin, you can dislike whomever you want. I need you to come get her."

Wait. Amy hates Piper? What's going on?

"Excuse me," I say.

Piper's mother freezes and turns around. "I'll call you back." She hangs up. "You're Amy's dad." She swallows.

"Amy doesn't hate your daughter, you know."

Piper's studying the carpet.

"Although if I were Amy, I would. If you had any idea how many times Amy came home crying because—" I clench my fist. "But if that's really what you believe, that's between you and your daughter." I shrug. "If you see Amy, please make sure your daughter leaves my spoiled brat alone and tell her that her rich as sin father is looking for her."

Piper's mother blinks.

I'm sure she's worried I'll tell Paul or Geo and she'll get fired. She should be nervous. Her daughter's awful and frankly, a menace. But maybe Mary was right—it does appear that the mother, at least, is struggling. She may not have handled things gracefully, but I haven't been under that particular type of pressure. Maybe I'd have been just as oblivious to my child's behavior or problems.

When I walk back outside, Amy's sitting on the ground by Lucy, leaning over the box and petting Hope. I hope she's not getting grass stains on her skirt. Mary always finds her the most beautiful dresses. This one goes with Trudy's green, blue, and purple theme perfectly, and stains would distress my already stressed-out wife. "Hey, kid."

"Hi Dad." Amy smiles at me.

"Can we chat for a second?"

She hops up. "Sure. Did you see? Hope is totally fine about the velvet cord with the ring on it being tied around her neck."

"Uh, great."

"She pecked at it for a little bit, but now she's leaving it alone."

"Okay."

Amy frowns. "Is something wrong?"

"So Piper is here," I say. "Her dad didn't come get her, and her mom doesn't seem to be having any luck getting anyone to come pick her up."

Her tiny shoulders fall and I want to march back and kick both Piper and her mother out. No matter how hard things are for them, they hurt my angel. Amy's nice to everyone. What kind of brat—

"It's fine," Amy says. "She won't be mean to me at my aunt's wedding."

"What?"

"She can stay. It's fine."

I clear my throat. "The thing is, she's not really dressed for a wedding." I don't mention that apparently her mother can't even afford an appropriate outfit.

"Oh." Amy's brow furrows. "I have a dress in my bag in the car that she can use."

"Why do you have a dress—"

"Because Mary made us pack those hospital bags like a month ago, remember?"

"Hospital bags?" What is she talking about?

"She was worried that if the baby came early, you might not know what to pack to take with us to Grandma's."

Mary's a genius. "There's a dress in yours?"

Amy nods. "In case it happened on a Saturday."

For church the next morning. "You don't mind if Piper borrows it?"

She shrugs. "If she knows it's mine, she might not want it."

"Then you'd better be the one to offer it to her."

Her eyes widen and she shakes her head. "Uh, no. That's a bad idea."

"I think it's a good idea." I take her hand in mine. "I'll come with you."

"Dad—"

I squeeze her hand. "Do you trust me?"

Amy nods.

"Okay, well, this isn't easy to say, okay? But I think Mary was right. She said that Piper and her mom might be having a hard time, and after hearing part of a phone conversation I shouldn't have heard, I think they are. If you don't make fun of her for it, she might ease up a bit. She might even realize that you're not her enemy."

Amy gulps. "Okay."

"Alright." I keep her hand in mine as we walk into Paul's house.

"Piper's mom," I say. "I don't know your name, I'm sorry."

"It's Lindzee," she says. "Lindzee Nickloh."

"It's nice to meet you, Lindzee," I say. "This is my daughter Amy."

"Hi," Amy says, pointedly not looking at Piper.

"Amy didn't realize Piper was here, but when I told her she wasn't dressed and that she might not feel like she fit in without appropriate clothing, she had an idea."

"I have a dress in my car," Amy says softly. "If you'd like to borrow it."

"Oh." Piper glances up at her mom, whose lips are tightly pursed. Her mom shrugs. "Okay. That would be really great."

Amy and I extricate the dress from the bag and bring it back. It's not quite as elaborate as the one Amy's wearing, but it's still very nice. Delicate embroidery runs across the bodice and down the skirt. "You can keep it," Amy says. "It's a little too short for me, but I bet it's perfect for you."

Amy's only an inch taller than Piper, but it was the perfect cover for a kind gesture. I've never been more proud. I watch Piper to see whether she's upset at all, but I only see gratitude.

I doubt this will transform her, but any cooling of tensions would be welcomed. "Alright, we better go take our seats," I say. "Especially since you have a chicken to prepare."

"A chicken?" Piper asks.

Amy beams. Nothing makes her happy like telling the story of Hope. She launches into it with the skill of a veteran storyteller. "And just last night," Amy says, "she ate her first piece of watermelon—on her own."

"That's cool," Piper says.

"And my mom says it's not a day too early," Amy says.

Her mom. It's the first time she's called Mary that in weeks. I close my eyes and pray that it's not a fluke.

"Alright." I offer Amy my hand. "Let's go."

Amy reaches the chicken just in time. Two minutes later, the wedding march starts, and I hurry up the aisle to sit next to Mary on the front row. Given Mary's advanced pregnancy, Trudy isn't making her wedding party line up for the ceremony. We both turn around to watch as Chase and Troy bean everyone in the aisle in the knee, the foot, the elbow and even the shoulder with flower petal wads.

Trudy knew this would happen.

I chuckle at it anyway.

And then Amy and her diapered, injured chicken walk down the aisle. That chicken rests its head right on Amy's chest, and my heart expands until it barely fits inside my chest. Mary did this—helped Amy to find the bravery to take such a big risk, and then nursed that chicken day in and day out, while pregnant and hosting my useless sister-in-law.

I lace my hands through hers. "Thank you," I say softly.

Mary leans against my shoulder. "For what?"

"For being you," I say. "For taking on everything that comes. For never complaining. For taking care of everyone around you. And most of all, for loving me."

Mary's eyes well with tears and she swats me again. "I'm not wearing waterproof mascara, Luke Manning, so shut your mouth."

"Whose fault is that?" I whisper back. "You're at your sister's wedding."

"My waterproof ran out," she hisses.

I shrug. "Not my fault."

And then Mary's eyes shift from my face upward, and I know Trudy's coming down the aisle, led by my beaming father. He didn't have a daughter to give away, so filling in for Trudy is a pretty big honor.

Trudy may not have the competency of Mary, but she has come so far in the past year and a half. She's beaming as she walks up the aisle, her smile turning into a laugh when she notices the piles of flower petals where there should be an evenly distributed layer. Ah, kids.

I spin in my chair to see my brother. He's staring at Trudy like he's on death row and she's his pardon. Like he's in freefall and she's the parachute.

"He's finally as pathetic as us," a deep voice behind me says.

I look over my shoulder at James Fulton the third and practically do a double take. "Paul invited you?"

James shakes his head with absolute mirth. "Not even close, but Trudy invited my delightful wife." Paisley waves. "And I'm her permanent plus one."

I laugh. When I met Mary at that bar, no one could have ever convinced me that James would be a guest at Paul's wedding, and my wife's sister would be marrying my brother. "I'm glad to see you looking so pathetic," I say. "It suits you."

"You wear it well too," James says.

And then the music stops, and the pastor starts yammering. "Did you prepare vows?" he finally asks.

"I did," Trudy says. "Should I go first?"

Paul shakes his head. "Heavens no. You always let the worst go first. Did you learn nothing in primary school?"

"Primary school?" Trudy laughs. "In America, we call that elementary school." She rolls her eyes. "Fine. You go first, mister bossy."

Paul beams. "Mister bossy. I imagine most of the guests know that the first time I met you, I was your boss. I'm pleased to say that you've been in charge ever since."

I chuckle.

"But I wouldn't have it any other way, because before I met you, I was utterly lost. Before I met you, I worried about things that didn't matter. I fretted over nonsense. Meeting you was what I needed—a kick in the pants to set me on the right path."

"Those are the vows you planned?" Trudy's eyebrow flies up. "It's not even a promise. It's just a statement—and not a flattering one. I'm not a kick in the pants, but I'll show you—"

"Let me finish," Paul says with a grin.

Trudy sighs. "If you think you can redeem yourself, go ahead."

"All these people are here for a wedding," Paul says. "There's even a miracle chicken. Did you see that?" He grins. "With all these guests watching, I better do a little better than just try." He takes her hand. "My vows to you are that you will always be my boss. You will always be my true north. You'll always be the light that helps me see what matters. And I promise that when I'm wrong, which still happens, you have my permission to kick me in the pants, any time you want. I won't even complain. Much."

Trudy rolls her eyes, but she's smiling. "That was a little better." She leans up on her tip toes and kisses him lightly.

"Hey, it's not time for that yet," the pastor objects.

"Did you hear what he said?" Trudy asks. "I'm the boss."

Mary laughs, and I chuckle again.

"In all seriousness though, my life was a disaster when I met you, Paul. I liked you immediately. Who wouldn't?" She looks around at the audience. "I mean, look at him."

Lots of ladies giggle.

"But I wouldn't even consider dating Paul Manning, partially because I didn't know you *were* Paul Manning, but also because I wasn't ready to date anyone yet. I thought I needed to graduate, find a good job, and get my debts repaid before I would be ready. In fact, I made a list, and I was determined to work my way through it before even considering a relationship."

"You did accomplish every single thing," Paul says. "On your own."

Trudy smiles, but it's all for Paul. "I did, and only then did I realize that my list was a waste of paper. You don't become ready to love someone because you've graduated from college, or because you have a job, or because you're financially secure." She touches his face. "In the process of doing those things, I learned to trust myself again. I learned that I was enough, and that confidence in myself allowed me to believe what you'd been telling me all along, that I was all you wanted. That I was good enough to love you, and that I could trust you to love me back."

Trudy turns toward the audience. "So if you're making lists and checking things off, take a good look at the things you're waiting on. Sometimes the real list you should be following has nothing to do with accomplishments. What you need is to develop a little faith in yourself. Paul waited while I restored mine, and it's his patience and his support that made him the one for me. Not this gorgeous face or this magnificent house. So my vow to you, Paul, is that I will keep on trusting you, and keep on supporting you, and keep on believing in you now, tomorrow, and next year, come what may. I'll believe in us forever."

"Now," the pastor says. "Now I pronounce you husband and wife and invite you to kiss."

And boy do they listen.

When they finally stop, Trudy looks right at Mary. "Who wants cake?"

All the guests cheer.

I stand up and offer Mary my hand. "My sweetheart."

She stands up slowly, one hand on her lower back. "My back is killing me—these chairs are horrible."

"Your back hurts?" I ask.

She nods.

And then liquid splashes on the ground. "Um, what was that?" I ask.

"I think my water just broke."

"What?" Paisley asks behind us. "Did you just say your water broke?"

Trudy's walking down the aisle, but she's close enough to hear it. "Whoa! Did you hear that?" She whoops. "My sister's having her baby!"

Mary shakes her head. "It's fine. Let's cut the cake."

My brand new sister-in-law shoves her way through the crowd. "You've lost your mind if you think a little cake is more important than supporting my sister or celebrating my nephew's birth."

She's not kidding.

"Can we get that cake to go?" Paul asks.

And it turns out, we can.

Mary's water broke like *the second* Aunt Trudy's wedding ended.

And then everyone went totally bonkers.

Aunt Trudy skipped her own cake and dancing and everything that happened at Dad's wedding. She didn't even toss the flowers, and I really wanted to catch them.

Hope and I just kind of stood in the middle of the chaos.

Piper's words circled around in my head like fish, swimming, swimming, swimming. Once she has a *real* kid, are you worried she won't like you anymore? Once she has a *real* kid, are you worried she won't like you anymore? Once she has a *real* kid, are you worried she won't like you anymore?

I'm not, or I wasn't. Not really.

Until everyone forgets I'm even here, and the baby hasn't even been born yet.

Lucy touches my shoulder. "Hey sweetie. You look a little lost."

"I guess my dad's going to the hospital."

"Are you going with them?"

I shrug.

"Let's find out what the plan is," she says. "And if you need a ride home, we'll definitely give you one. I'm also happy to stay with you as long as you need me to."

"What about Chase?" I'm not sure where he is, since I had Hope and he and Troy went in front of me.

"I think he's with Trudy and Troy." Lucy points. "Is that your cousin's name?"

I nod.

"Let's hurry over there and ask your aunt what she thinks."

Coach Brian is really great, shoving people aside like he played football instead of baseball. Actually, maybe he played that too. We reach Trudy in record time, even though she's surrounded by guests wishing her well as she tries to escape.

"Aunt Trudy," I say.

"Amy!" Trudy grabs me and pulls me against her snowy, bead-covered dress. "I told your dad to take Mary right to the hospital and I'd bring you and Troy."

"We're going?" Excitement bubbles inside my chest.

Trudy smiles kindly, but she shakes her head. "Well, we have no idea how long having that baby will take. So for now, I meant that we'll take you to your house. But of course, once the baby is born, you'll be first in line to meet him. Your dad says he texted your aunt. She says she'll be delighted to watch you and Chase tonight."

"I'm headed back there anyway," Lucy offers. "I can take them, if that helps. You can cut the cake and dance a song or something in the time you would have been driving over."

Aunt Trudy laughs. "I don't care about all that, not nearly as much as I care about being there for Mary." She drops her voice a bit. "It's scary, having your first baby, and she was there with me."

Lucy nods. "Alright, but the offer still stands."

Aunt Trudy glances down at me. "What do you think, munchkin? You nervous? Do you need your aunt to take you home?"

It helps that she asked—that she cares if I'm okay. So I shake my head. "Me and Chase are good. We like Lucy, and she's good with Hope, too."

My aunt cocks her eyebrow. "Are you saying I can't handle a chicken? My very own feathered assistant ring bearer?"

"No."

"Aren't you just Miss Serious. Oh fine, let's get the car seats moved over, and I'll let Lucy take you home."

In the car, Lucy tries really hard to talk to me and Chase, but Chase keeps singing "Slippery Fish" over and over, and I don't really feel like talking. Eventually she starts talking to Coach Brian. They drove over together, and watching them smile and talk makes me happier.

But by the time we reach the house, I'm back to thinking about why I'm here with no Dad and no Mary.

My stepmom is about to have another baby.

Her baby.

Her *real* baby.

My half-brother, the kid who's actually half of Mary.

As if she knows I'm having a bad day, Aunt Anica's waiting on the front porch. "Hey guys—I hear Mary ruined the wedding." Her attempt at a joke reminds me that half of me is probably like her, instead of being like Mary. Mean, lazy, and always grumpy.

"Actually, I've never seen Aunt Trudy happier," I say, pushing past Aunt Anica.

"Hey, Amy?" Lucy's voice is so soft I almost don't hear her.

I turn back. "Yeah?"

"Thank you." Her smile is small, but she glances back at her car where Coach Brian is waiting.

I grin. "He cares about other people," I say. "That's what you said you wanted."

Lucy puts one hand to her neck. "He really does, *and* he's handsome. And smart. So, really, thank you."

"You're welcome."

"Alright," Aunt Anica says. "Time to head inside." She seems even grumpier than usual, but I have no idea why.

"We're supposed to be eating cake," I say. "Sorry if we're not marching to our rooms fast enough for you."

I expect Aunt Anica to snap at me. I do not expect her to lean her head back and roar with laughter.

"What's so funny?" I cross my arms and lean against the closed front door.

"You." She shakes her head. "You're so much like Mary that sometimes I forget how much Lizzie is in there, too."

Great, so when I'm rude, I am like my mom. And if I make Aunt Anica happy, I hurt Mary. If I make Mary happy, I hurt Aunt Anica, and if she's watching me from up in heaven, maybe my mom, too.

It's all so confusing and unfair.

I'm the one who doesn't have a mom, but somehow everyone is mad at me for it.

I run past Aunt Anica and keep going, all the way to my room. Then I slam the door and fall onto the bed, bawling like a baby into my pillow. I'm not sure if I'm mad or sad or something else, but whatever is wrong, it's too much, and I want it to go away.

A few minutes later, I hear the opening song from *Paw Patrol* blaring in the family room. Looks like Aunt Anica has plugged Chase in, probably so she can go take a nap in her room.

The tap at my door surprises me, and I sit up and wipe at my wet cheeks.

I don't say anything, but the door opens anyway. Aunt Anica's blonde head pokes through. "Amy?" Her eyes meet mine. "Can I come in? Or will you throw something?"

"I wouldn't want to break any of my toys on your hard head," I say.

She laughs again, but this time it's a small laugh. "Will you talk to me?"

I shrug. "It's a free country."

"Less and less every day," Anica says.

I frown. "What does that mean?"

"Never mind." She sits on the edge of my bed. "Look, kid. I've been a terrible aunt, and a terrible friend, and well, kind of a horrible person. You were right at school. I think I needed to listen to my mom's lessons a little better as a kid."

"I was right?"

She nods and scoots a little closer. "You were totally right. And Mary was right. And I was wrong."

I sniffle and wipe at my nose. "About what?"

"Well, first, I need to apologize for what I said the night I arrived."

"What?"

"You called Mary 'Mom.'"

I twist my hands together. "I haven't done it since then." Except I might have slipped up once or twice, but not around Mary or Aunt Anica, for sure.

"I know," Aunt Anica says, "and that's on me. I am way late talking to you about this. I guess hearing you—knowing it hurt Mary—well, somehow it made me feel better. I really am a terrible person."

I open my mouth, but she picks up her hand and shushes me.

"No, let me finish. I knew that I shouldn't have said what I did. I knew Lizzie—your mom—would be furious with me for chastising you. You probably don't remember a lot about her. You were really young when she died, but I can tell you this. She would *not* have wanted you to be sad. She's—" Aunt Anica starts to cry. But she takes huge, gulping breaths. "She would be so happy that you found Mary for Luke, and for you and Chase. Her biggest fear when she got sick was that you wouldn't have a mother. She told me that, and I. . ." Aunt Anica pulls me against her for a hug.

I stiffen a little bit. I can't help it. She lied to me.

Finally, she lets me go. "I did what I did because I was selfish and I was hurting."

Just like Mary said. People who are mean to other people are usually like that because they're hurting themselves.

"Every time I wanted to tell you that I was wrong and that it was okay for you to love Mary, every time I almost told you that I was glad you had someone, I got upset that I still don't have anyone. Not a friend, not a boyfriend, no one."

"Maybe if you woke up a little earlier you might meet someone," I say. "But you do have me." It's hard, but I make myself hug her. I think both of my moms would want me to.

She laughs, again. I really do not understand her at all. "You're an amazing kid," she says. "You're kind, you're brave, you're resilient, and my sister, she could not possibly be any prouder of you, I promise. But you also have an amazing mom right here, in this house. She loves you as much as Lizzie did, and she will do anything for you. I've seen that, time and again over the past few weeks." Her voice drops to a whisper. "And even though Mary had things kind of hard, she's handled them with so much more grace than I have."

"Now she's having a baby."

"She sure is, right now, maybe." Aunt Anica smiles at me.

I duck my head so she won't notice that I'm not excited. But I'm too late, I guess.

"Hey, what's wrong?"

I shake my head. "Nothing."

She lifts my chin up. "Something."

"It's something that Piper said."

"That little brat." She mutters something I can't understand under her breath. "Did it get worse?"

I shrug. "Not really."

"Then what did she say?"

"She said. . ." I close my eyes. "She said once Mary has a real baby, she won't. . ."

"Mary won't love you anymore?" Aunt Anica dips down until she's looking at me. "You don't believe that, right?"

I shrug again. "I don't know."

This time, she doesn't laugh. "My sister was fantastic. She was brave and bold and she took no prisoners. But in her own way, your Mary is just as fierce. And I've never been more positive that someone loved her daughter than I am about Mary's love for you. She could have a hundred more babies and she wouldn't love you less, because she loves you all the way."

I hiccup.

Then I can't seem to stop hiccupping.

Aunt Anica hugs me really tight, almost too tight, but I don't stop her. "I've said a lot of dumb things since coming to visit," she says. "But believe me when I tell you this. Your new mom loves you with every single speck of her body. Mary may be tired and busy over the next few weeks, but that idiot Piper has never been more wrong."

I want to believe Aunt Anica so badly. When I go to bed that night, I don't even have the nightmare I've been having, that Mary sends me to live with Grandma and

Grandpa after the new baby comes home. The next morning, Aunt Anica doesn't bother taking us to church, but she does dress Chase and me in nice enough clothes to go meet the new baby at the hospital.

"Mom will be back tomorrow," Aunt Anica says. "She and Dad didn't come back for me, but they're coming home a few days early to watch you two angels now that your dad's having a new baby. Apparently they don't trust me to keep you alive."

"When is Daddy coming back?" Chase asks as Aunt Anica buckles him into his car seat.

"Probably not for a few days," she says. "Are you upset?"

"You put orange juice in my Cocoa Puffs," Chase says. "It was gross."

"Hey, I loved that when I was a kid," Aunt Anica says. "If you'd give it a chance you might love it too."

Chase curls his lip and stares out the window of the car.

When we reach the hospital, all the things Aunt Anica said about Mary seem kind of... not believable. My heart starts to beat super fast. What if Aunt Anica's wrong? What if Mary's so happy with this new baby that she's sick of dealing with me?

But when we go into the room, Mary's eyes light up. She sits up in the bed, a little pink baby resting in the elbow of one arm. "Come meet your new brother," she says. "You can hop up on the bed with me so you can really see him."

I walk forward slowly, watching Mary more than the baby. But when I get close, he coos. The little pink guy squirms and makes this little bubbly coo sound and something inside me softens and I can't help myself. He might ruin everything, and my life may never be the same, but still. In spite of all of that. . .

I like him.

"What's his name?" Chase asks.

Dad stands up and walks around behind us. "We decided to name him Dragon."

Mary rolls her eyes.

"That's a really good name," Chase says, his eyes wide. Then he frowns. "Hey, how come he gets a good name and mine is just boring old Chase?"

"Dad's kidding," I say. "What did you really name him?"

"This is your brother, Jack," Mary says with a twinkle in her eyes. "Jack Harold Manning."

"Harold, like Grandpa Harold?" I ask.

Mary nods. "Yes, just like that."

"I bet he's happy," I say.

"We hope so," Dad says.

"Do you want to hold him?" Mary asks.

I look up to meet her eyes. "Hold him?"

"If you sit right next to me on the bed, you can hold him."

I nod, surprised that I actually do want to hold him. And when Mary puts him on my lap and her arm around me, I like him even more. Then, for a super short moment, he smiles at me. "Hey," I say.

"Did you see that, Luke?" Mom squeezes my shoulders with her arm. "He likes her."

And for the first time since Mom and Dad ran away from Aunt Trudy's wedding, I'm pretty sure Mom still likes me too.

AMY

Mom stays at the hospital for four days after Jack's born, but thankfully Grandma and Grandpa take over for Aunt Anica the day after we visit the hospital.

"You were a brave little girl," Grandma says.

"I was?"

"You survived your Aunt Anica's cooking." Grandma smiles.

Aunt Anica looks annoyed. "I'm not that bad."

"She burned my toast this morning," Chase says. "Until it was black."

Grandma laughs. "The Maggard family isn't known for being great in the kitchen."

Aunt Anica stands up.

"I assume you'll be headed for my house?" Grandma asks.

"No." Aunt Anica frowns.

"No?" Grandma plants both her hands on the countertop and leans forward. "What's your plan then? Are you so mad at us for taking a vacation that you're headed back to San Francisco the second we come home?"

Aunt Anica shakes her head. "Luke said I'm welcome here as long as I want to stay."

"They have a new baby," Grandma says. "He's being polite. Do you really think they want a houseguest?"

She shrugs. "Maybe."

"Forget Luke. Do you think Mary wants the sister of her husband's first wife staying with her?"

"If they don't want me here, you can be sure I'll pack up and head to your very welcoming home right away."

Grandma laughs, and Aunt Anica storms out of the kitchen.

At least I get to go to school most of the day, and I spend the hours after I get home with Hope in the backyard. At first she's really happy to be outside, but then it kind of seems like she's looking for something. She keeps clucking, over and over. "What's wrong?" I ask Hope, wishing she could answer me.

"I think she might be lonely," Aunt Anica says softly through her open window.

"I'm sorry. Am I too loud?" I gather Hope next to me. "I didn't know your window was open."

"You have such a beautiful home," she says.

"No matter what Grandma says, I don't think Mom and Dad will care if you stay as long as you're nice." I swallow. "And if you don't get mad that I call Mary 'Mom.'"

She laughs. "I think we've established that even if I do care, that's my problem and not yours."

"Hey, have you been changing Hope's towels and food and water?"

"Maybe." She shrugs. "She's a cute chicken. What can I say? She's grown on me."

My cute chicken walks past, and I pet her—which makes her huddle down next to me, clucking much more quietly. "Do you really think she's lonely?"

"I looked it up online," she says. "The website I found

says that chickens are very social. Chase keeps asking for chicks. Since you want to keep her, she'll need a coop and a few friends too. Chicks might not be a bad idea."

"I don't think she likes being in the box anymore," I say.

"Why not?"

"Well." I glance around to make sure Grandma isn't out here. She's not a fan of Hope. "Um, she keeps hopping out of it and following me to the door every night."

Aunt Anica laughs. "And I thought she liked me, but she never follows me anywhere."

"I think she likes you just fine."

"Well, that's good to know. Makes me feel like a little less of a loser."

"You're not a loser. Dad says you're kind of famous." Which he also told me not to tell her. Whoops.

She shakes her head. "I'm not even close to famous."

But since I already said something. . . "Hey, how come you don't write books anymore?"

She freezes.

"Is that a mean thing to ask?" I bite my lip. "I'm sorry if it is. You don't have to tell me, but Dad said you *used* to write books. Like you don't do it anymore. I think if I wrote books that people liked, I'd keep doing it."

"Words used to just pile up inside of me." She inhales and leans against the windowsill. "I used to see the world differently. My first book told a story about a girl to whom many bad things happened, but in spite of those, the ending was 'surprisingly hopeful,' or that's what the *New York Times* said."

"But all the words went away?"

"Something like that," she says. "And now I want to write again, but everything is all jumbled."

I stand up and pick up Hope. "Maybe you needed more friends, like Hope does. Maybe the words are all mixed up because you're keeping too many of them inside you. If you weren't so lonely, it might be easier to write more books."

Aunt Anica doesn't laugh this time. She just stares at me. "You know, you're awfully smart for a little thing. You might actually be right."

"Then it's good you want to stay here. There are a lot of people here, like all the time. Plus, you know, you have me."

"And I'm really glad I have you. You know that, right?"

I beam at her. "Yep, I do now."

When Mom and Dad and Jack come home, the house *really* has a lot going on all the time. That sweet little baby who just smiled up at me seems to cry more than he does anything else. And he eats and burps and poops a lot, so that's saying something.

"Do you think he has colic?" Luke asks. "Amy and Chase didn't cry like this."

"Babies can't have colic until they're at least a month old," Mary says, her voice all tight and kinda mad sounding.

"Someone should tell Jack that," Dad says, walking back and forth and bouncing the whimpering baby.

I offer to help, but they tell me it's fine.

It's a good thing Aunt Anica stays, because now that the baby is home, she helps a lot. Like, way more than she ever did before.

She vacuums.

She takes me to school.

She makes toast. Kind of burned toast, but it's not as black as before.

She even picks me up after play practice.

"Hey, how's that wretched Piper doing?" she asks on Wednesday. "Any better?"

I shrug.

"So no."

"She's not mean anymore. She just pretends I don't exist at all, mostly."

"That's an improvement, I guess."

I can't disagree, but I wish I hadn't given her my dress.

When we get back to the house, Lucy's walking up the sidewalk, and she's carrying a box. "Amy!" She waves.

I roll down the window. "Hey!" After Aunt Anica parks Mom's car, I hop out and run around to the side door so I can help her. "What's this?"

"It's a baby gift," she says, her face looking kind of funny.

"That's a big box," I say.

"Well, it's a weird gift. If your parents don't like it, they don't have to take it."

Something inside the box makes noise, and I almost drop it.

"What's that?"

Lucy smiles. "You'll see."

We set the box down, and I open the door. "Mom!" I call. "Mom, Lucy's here, and she has a present for you."

"For all of you, actually." Lucy picks the box up again, and she shifts it. Then she shifts it again. This time, I recognize the sound it makes.

It's definitely a cluck.

"Did you bring us a chicken?" I whisper.

"Shh," she says, faking a frown. "Don't ruin the surprise."

She's a strange lady.

Mom comes into the room without a baby in her arms for once.

"Where's Jack?" I ask.

"He's actually asleep, wonder of wonders." She yawns. "Lucy, great to see you." Mom looks tired, so tired, all the time, but she forces a smile.

"I know you're busy and tired and probably don't have time right now." Lucy pats the box. "But, well, Amy told

Brian that Hope is hopping all over and that maybe she's lonely."

Mom's head cuts toward mine. "She's lonely? What's wrong?"

I shrug. "It's fine."

"You have to tell me when something's wrong," she scolds. "I'm too tired to notice anything on my own right now." She drops a hand on the top of my head.

"Well, I have an old coop that I haven't used in a few months, not since I got a bigger one. I kept it in case I ever needed to quarantine any birds, or for when I got chicks again, but I'm not using it now... and I thought I might offer to loan it to you. At least until you can figure out what you want to use. I also brought Hope's two best friends over. They've been complaining ever since she left, and having two more adult chickens means you won't have to worry about dealing with chicks right now."

Mom starts to cry.

"Oh no," Lucy says. "I'm so sorry. If this is too much, I can take them home. I can even take Hope with me, if it's too stressful."

Mom shakes her head. "It's not too much. I'm grateful. We love Hope, and I'm too tired right now to go pick a coop and chicks and heat lamps. Just looking it all up made me want to break down." She wipes at her eyes. "I'm a mess. I'm sorry. What a kind gesture."

"So we can keep them?" I bounce up and down on my toes.

"I can send Luke over later to get the coop." Mom crosses the room and hugs Lucy.

"Oh, don't worry about that. Brian will be over soon, and he can bring it."

Mom's eyes light up, and she lets Lucy go. "Brian's coming over?"

"He comes over most days now." Lucy drops down on

her knees. "And listen, I just wanted to tell your brilliant daughter thank you again. I've never been this happy."

I pat Andy on the head. "So maybe she knew what she was doing that night."

Lucy presses a kiss against my forehead. "I think someone knew what they were doing. Maybe it was Andy. Or maybe it was someone a little bit smarter. Who knows?"

Hope is giddy when we release her into the backyard with her friends—a brownish red chicken called a Rhode Island Red and black and white striped hen called a Cuckoo Marans. They'll need actual names soon, but I love them already. And just like Lucy said he would, Coach Brian brings the coop over a few minutes later. Hope runs toward it almost immediately, her two friends fluttering after her.

"The Rhode Island Red looks so funny when she gets excited," I say. "Like a lady with a big old dress, trying to lift it up and run."

"She does look a little like that," Dad says, waving to Coach Brian. "Thanks for bringing that over. We appreciate the loan."

"Lucy sure loves her chickens," he says. "So the fact that she trusts you with not one, but three of them, means she really has a lot of faith in you, Amy."

I offer a handful of mealworms to Hope. As soon as she starts eating, her two friends run over. They're a lot more nervous to be near me, but not nervous enough to turn down dried mealworms.

"I thought you were a little nutty when you asked me to come see this chicken at school that day," Coach Brian says. "But I didn't quite know how to say no, so I came."

"Oh." I stand up and brush off my hands. "Well, I'm glad you did."

His smile is so wide I can see all his teeth *and* all his gums. "I am too. So glad."

I'm still smiling when I help Dad set up the food and

water for our three new chickens. And I spend the next hour or so making sure that Andy will be as nice to them as she is to Hope.

The next few days go by in a blur, and then on Friday, it's time for our dress rehearsal, where we put on our actual costumes and pretend there's an audience. I'm dressed and waiting on the side of the curtain when I hear someone say "Psst."

I turn to look across the stage, and it's the last person I expect to be talking to me.

Piper.

"What?" I hiss back.

"Come here." She waves me over.

The curtain could come up at any time. Except, I notice she's not in her costume. I run across the stage as quietly as I can.

"What's going on?" I ask.

She shakes her head. "I'm sick. My throat hurts, so I can't sing."

I blink. "Are you kidding?"

"No."

"You sound fine."

"My throat hurts, okay?"

"You sounded fine in choir today."

"It's new," she says. "And it hurts real bad."

I frown. "So we're not having the play?"

She shrugs. "You know my lines."

"How do you know that?"

"Because when I forget them, you always tell me what to say."

I roll my eyes. "I have a part already."

"You should have been Annie." She crosses her arms. "I heard Coach Brian say that."

I put one hand on my hip. "You're a good Annie, and I like being Mrs. Hannigan."

She looks at the ground. "What if I mess up?"

Is Piper. . . scared? "You won't."

"I will," she says. "I forget my lines all the time. I'm not like you."

"So if you do, then you think about the next scene, and you just make up whatever you need to say to get there."

"How come you're so smart?" Piper looks up and meets my eyes.

"You're smart too."

She shakes her head. "Not really. Math is hard, and so is writing. And I hate school."

I had no idea she hated school. She's like the queen of school.

"Besides, I don't think my mom can come."

Is she kidding? "I don't think my mom can come either." As I say the words, I realize they're probably true. Mom hasn't left the house since Jack was born, and she always seems so tired. "She just had a baby."

"I'm sorry," Piper says, "that I said she won't like you anymore."

"She does love me still," I say.

Piper nods. "I know."

"It did make me sad, but I figured it out."

"My dad doesn't." Her words are barely a whisper.

"What?" I step closer.

"My dad got married again, and he had another baby, and now he never comes to see me. But he wasn't very good before, and your mom is pretty amazing."

Oh no. Mom was right. She was *so* right. I don't even think—I just do it. I wrap my arms around her and squeeze. "Your throat doesn't hurt. Your heart hurts, and I've had that happen to me too."

Piper hugs me back for a minute, and then she steps back. "Can you not tell anyone that I asked you to be Annie for me, please?"

She doesn't ask me not to talk about her dad or the fact that her mom's not coming, but I know she's asking about all of it. "I won't say anything."

She ducks back behind the curtain and disappears.

A few minutes later, she shows up again, this time in costume, and the dress rehearsal starts. She doesn't forget a single line.

"You've all worked so hard," Mrs. Tassain says. "I couldn't be more proud of you. I really think this is going to be the best second grade play I have ever seen."

"It's your first one, isn't it?" Coach Brian asks. "I thought that until this year, they only did plays for fifth, fourth, and third."

"Shh," she says with a big smile. "That's beside the point. I am so impressed with all of you."

Even though I know all the lines in the entire play by heart, on Saturday morning, I decide to review the script one last time, just to make sure. I mean, if I need to help Piper or someone else, I better be super sure I'm right.

I'm sitting in the back yard with Hope, Rita, and KoKo Krispy—five year olds should not be allowed to name chickens, even if they need to feel like they're involved—when I hear a car pull up in the driveway. "I'll be back." I put Hope down and run through the gate to see Aunt Paisley.

"Hey kid," she says. "How's your mom?"

I shrug. "She's tired. The baby cries a lot."

Aunt Paisley laughs. "All babies cry a lot."

"But this one's worse. Dad thinks he might be broken." I stand up super straight. "I never cried this much, he says."

"Alright, alright, well, walk me inside, will you? That way your huge dog-bear won't bite me."

"Andy wouldn't bite you," I say. "She might lick you to death though."

"I'd prefer to avoid that, too." Paisley follows me inside.

"Mom!" I shout. "Aunt Paisley's here."

I don't listen to the entire conversation, because they tend to get super boring, but from what I gather, Paisley quit her job when Mom left.

"You have to do it," she says really loudly and with a ton of energy. "Luke's right. I'll come with you, of course. James wants me to take time off, but if I do that, I'll never go back. I'll get sucked into the whole New York City scene and I'll be subsumed, I just know it."

Mom shakes her head. "I don't like being a boss. I like doing tax returns. They're simple, and they have right and wrong answers."

"But it's *boring*," Aunt Paisley says. "And you're such a great boss. All the things that are worth doing are hard, but that doesn't mean we shouldn't do them. You're just saying that because you have a newborn. Don't make big decisions while you're sleep deprived."

Mom snorts. "So I should decide to open my own firm with you while I'm sleep deprived?"

"Sorry, let me rephrase. Don't make bad decisions when you're sleep deprived. Let your friends guide you so that you make good ones."

"How's this?" Mom says. "You come back next week and we'll hammer out some preliminary details of what it would even look like. That'll give me another week to get this baby thing all figured out."

"And if James and I send you a night nurse as a baby gift, maybe you'll be in a frame of mind to do just that," Aunt Paisley says. "Tell me you'd accept it."

Mom stands up. "It's a generous offer."

"You don't have a mom to help, and your sister's on a honeymoon. Let me give you a night nurse for a few weeks." She slings an arm around Mom. "Please."

"Fine," Mom says.

I sneak off to my room after that, smiling. I do like

baby Jack, even though he cries a lot. But I'll like him more when he's not making Mom so tired.

The next day, Aunt Anica volunteers to take me to the school—since I have to be there an hour before the play starts. "Thanks," Dad says.

"Happy to help," she says.

"Speaking of." Dad glances at me as if he has just noticed I'm there, listening.

I think he wants me to go away so he can ask Aunt Anica something interesting, but I'm tired of missing out of things, so I pretend I don't know what he wants.

"It's fine," Aunt Anica says. "You can say anything you want in front of the kiddo. We're cool."

"Well, I talked to Mary. We're happy to have you stay here in a more long-term way, especially if you're willing to do the chores we discussed. It would be a huge help, honestly."

"Thanks," she says. "It means a lot."

"And I'm glad you can have this time with the kids," Dad says. "I'd rather have you helping out than someone they don't even know."

"Me too." She grabs my shoulder and ushers me out to the car.

Once we reach the school, she asks, "Need me to stay with you?"

"Nah," I say. "I'll be fine."

"Are you sure?" She shuffles toward the door to the choir room where we're gathering. "Because I've got some real zingers ready if Piper's feeling sassy."

"Actually," I say. "I think we might be doing a little better. Mom was really right—she's kind of not very happy right now."

"Alright. But if you need me, I'm here." Anica pulls me against her side, pressing me against her with one arm, and then she walks off.

While Mrs. Tassain adjusts our costumes and Coach Brian has us run through some speaking drills, I wonder.

Will Dad be able to get away? Will they bring Chase? What about Aunt Anica? I should have asked so I'd know. But I was afraid. Because I bet Dad comes for sure, but Dad has seen me in plays before. Christmas pageants. Last year's choir performance.

But I've never had a mom come. Never.

When the curtain goes up, the lights are so bright that it's hard to see who's in the audience. So I just pretend that none of them could make it. That way I won't be sad if they aren't here. Or, not as sad.

I sing and sing. I give my lines as loud and as rude as I can manage, just like Coach Brian said I should. Piper does a really good job too, just flubbing one little part, and I'm sure no one notices.

And when it's over, there's so much clapping it almost makes me want to cover my ears. My smile is so wide that my cheeks ache. When Piper hugs me, I almost fall over. "Thanks," she says. "And I'm sorry."

The lights finally fade, and I blink and blink.

Piper's mom actually came, but it doesn't look like anyone else she knows did. I want to tell her that it's okay, because the mom is the most important one. She's the one that really matters.

But I don't say anything, because then Coach Brian is telling me what a great job I did, and Lucy is standing next to him, her arm through his. They're both beaming at me, and Lucy even brought me flowers. "We wanted to congratulate you before you're completely drowning in people," Lucy says.

I have no idea what she's saying until Dad yells, "Whoa! Hey, everybody, is that? No!" He shakes his head. "It can't be! Is that THE Amy Manning?! The one who gave the most amazing performance of Mrs. Hannigan that has ever been seen?! I hear they're begging her to do the next Spielberg movie!"

I roll my eyes. My dad is so weird. "Hi Dad."

"It's definitely her," Aunt Anica says. "I just can't believe my eyes." She holds out a bouquet of flowers, Grandma and Grandpa walking around her to pick me up and hug me, passing me back and forth between them.

When they put me down, Chase barrels into me, planting a messy kiss on my cheek. "Good job." He laughs. "I really liked when you threw them into a big pile of dirty laundry. You were so mean."

I smile. I do have a pretty good brother. I'm surprised he sat through the whole thing. "Thanks for coming."

"That was the most amazing performance I've ever seen—especially from second graders." A familiar female voice. I turn fast, but it's only Aunt Paisley and her husband James. I force a smile as they hand me more flowers. And then Geo and her husband Trig hug me too. And even Geo's friend Rob comes. "Amazing job," he says. "I was floored."

"Thanks." My lip wobbles, but at least I don't cry. I'm sure Dad recorded it, and Mom can watch that later maybe.

"Amy!" This time, I know it's her. I turn toward the back of the auditorium and watch, wide-eyed as Mom jogs down the aisle, baby Jack in her arms. "Sorry, dear heart, he needed to eat, but I made him wait until it was over, so I had to rush out the second the curtain dropped."

She's crying. My mom saw my play, and she's crying.

"It was the most amazing thing I've ever watched. You have a real gift."

And then I'm crying too. Mom passes baby Jack to Dad and crouches down so I can hug her, my arms too tight around her neck, but I can't seem to help it. "Thanks."

"I wouldn't have missed this for anything," she whispers.

I believe her.

Because she's my real mom. And that's what moms do.

When everyone heads out of the theater, my arms full of flowers, I pause for just a second. And it's almost like someone else hugs me and presses a kiss to my cheek.

It might sound crazy, so I don't tell anyone else, but. . .

For the first time in my life, I wonder whether I might be the luckiest girl in the world. Because I'm pretty sure I have two moms who loved me enough to watch my play, not just one.

❧

Finding Peace, the last Finding Home Series book, is out now. And if you have time to review any or all of my Finding Books, on ANY platform (booksellers, Good-Reads, BookBub, you name it!) ALL reviews really help me. <3

And if you like talking with other people who have read the series, join my reader group on Facebook here: https://www.facebook.com/groups/750807222376182. It's called Bridget E. Baker's Binge Reader Recovery Program, but I doubt it will really help you recover if you have a reading problem. . . Also, I'm working on writing some exclusive short stories for each of my series that I'll only make available in that group. So if you'd like to grab those, head on over.

I'm also including a sample chapter of Already Gone next, a standalone romantic suspense I wrote. I hope you'll keep on scrolling and check it out. It's not quite as heart-warming as the Finding Series, but I think it will touch on many of the same things—family, decisions we make, and the things that matter most.

SAMPLE OF ALREADY GONE

* Lacy*

Time's a fickle trickster.

If I'd been born a few weeks earlier, I'm pretty sure it wouldn't have happened. If my vivacious little sister had been born a few weeks later, it might not have taken place. If Mason had shown up just one day after he did, it probably could've been avoided. If the principal had waited a few minutes that day, well, I don't know. Sometimes I think if I could've scraped together a handful of leftover seconds, we could've saved her.

She might still be alive.

❦

It's Hope's fault that I'm here, but I can't focus on that, not right now.

I'm supposed to sign in when I arrive at the shrink's

office. The little white sheet with blank spaces stares at me accusingly, like it knows what I've done. I want to sign in with a beautiful curly script, as if somehow that will make things better. I can't do it though, because there isn't a pen or pencil in sight. What kind of crappy, rundown office doesn't have a pen by the sign in sheet?

When I lean over to pull one out of my backpack, I unzip the front pocket too far. Pens and pencils scatter all over the faux-wood, scuffed laminate floors.

I want to swear, but I bite my tongue instead. Who knows what this secretary might tell the doctor? I really need him to write a positive evaluation for the court. Pens and pencils scattered all over the place, one shiny yellow number two pencil broke about a third of the way down. I stare at it dumbly, transfixed.

I broke it. Like I break everything.

The secretary walks around the counter to help me, and I notice she's wearing the exact same orthopedic sandals as my grandma. I wish Granny could still work in an office, instead of just laying in bed in a nursing home.

"Oh dear," the secretary mutters. "I do this kind of thing all the time. Here, let me help."

My conscience kicks me when she crouches down and starts gathering my clumsily scattered pens and pencils. I don't deserve her help. I don't deserve anyone's help.

I lean over to pick them up myself. "It's your fault this happened. Who doesn't have a pen out for the sign in sheet?"

She straightens up and glares at me. "Excuse me for helping."

I sigh. I should be thanking her, not yelling at her. My hands shake as I gather up the rest of my writing utensils, but I can't force out an apology. It's a good thing my mom's not here. She'd be furious.

I pick up the broken pencil and scrawl my name on the

white sheet with it, scrunching my fingers to make the little nub work.

"I am sorry I didn't have a pen out." The secretary holds out a blue ink pen and when I reach for it, she smiles. I notice she has lipstick on her teeth. I tap meaningfully on my tooth with the pathetic shard of my yellow pencil while she's looking at me. She inhales quickly and rubs on her tooth. "Did I get it?"

I shake my head.

"I'll just duck into the bathroom for a second."

I raise my eyebrows at her leaving me here unsupervised but don't stop her. After all, I know I'm not really a lunatic.

While she's cleaning the lipstick off, I glance around. The larger, shattered end of my pencil lies on the floor alone. I ought to pick it up and stick it in my bag. With a little sharpening, it'll be fine.

I wish people could be repaired as easily as writing utensils. Resharpened when we get dull, a little pink cap slapped on our heads when our factory erasers run down. I could use a little sharpening, too. In their own way, humans are more fragile than a pencil, and when we break, you can't just sharpen the shards and keep on writing.

The desk plaque for the younger-than-Granny secretary reads: Melinda. There's a stack of office supply order forms in front of her and I think about checking a box for some new pens as a joke. When I lean over it, something beneath it catches my eye. It pokes out from under the order forms, and I can barely make out the font at first. When I tilt my head, I realize it's a rèsumè, Melinda Brackenridge's résumé. I know why I want to escape this tiny office, since my butt was court-ordered to come in the first place, but why does she want to leave?

I hear the bathroom door and jump, straightening guiltily.

"How long have you worked for Dr. Brasher?" I ask to distract her from the guilty trembling of my hands.

"Oh, years and years now. First we were at a group practice, but they made him take a lot of patients he wasn't too happy with. He likes helping kids and teens. He started his own practice so he can do what he wants. You'll like him. Everyone does."

Somehow I doubt if he left a group practice to be a do-gooder. I bet he got fired or something and tells people he left to help kids. Sounds a lot better. "So he's what? A saintly shrink?"

Melinda's eyebrows draw together and her lips compress. "Dr. Brasher is the best child psychiatrist in the state."

"Then why do you want to leave him?"

Her jaw drops.

I point at the résumé.

Her face blanches. "I don't want to leave, I swear. Please don't say anything. He's such a good guy, and an amazing doctor."

I raise my eyebrows.

"I haven't had a pay raise in years and my son, well, I need a raise." She gulps.

If she meant to say that out loud, I'll eat my broken pencil, but I kind of like her more now. "Family should always come first."

She nods.

Family is complicated.

If it weren't for my little sister Hope, I doubt I'd be in this fusty old office, waiting on a shrink whose evaluation will determine whether I'm capable of being released into the world as an adult. And yet, the thought doesn't make me nearly as angry as it would have last week. I don't think I realized how much time I wasted being angry with Hope.

So many seconds thrown away. I wish I could gather

them up and hug them close. I wish I realized then that you can't hug people forever.

Melinda snags the clipboard and reads my name. Or she tries to, I think. So much for making a good first impression. "Angelique Vincent?"

I clear my throat. "Umm, I should be on the schedule. Lacy Shelton? I have a three-thirty appointment."

She squints at the tiny words on her paperwork. "Shelton. Yes, there you are. Let me see if he's ready." She ducks through the doorway that I assume leads to Dr. Brasher. When she opens the paneled wooden door again, she waves me over.

Melinda looks frazzled and guilty when I walk past, which is one emotion I recognize easily. It's obvious she doesn't want to quit, and I'm guessing she can't bring herself to ask for more money either. I wish I could help, but I don't have time to worry about her problems. Mine are about to slap me between the eyes.

For a moment Dr. Brasher meets my eyes silently. I stare right back. He's a tall man to be wearing that particular sweater vest. Before he sits down, I notice it isn't quite long enough. His hairy belly isn't something I particularly wanted to see, but I imagine he spends all day staring at people he'd rather not. I guess we all do junk we don't want to.

He looks down at a file sitting on his desk, and I follow his gaze to a photo of me and Hope, both of us smiling on a blanket on the beach. It's torn down the middle, and taped back together. I know who taped it. And I know she's gone now, never to return. Like a pencil in a wood chipper, irreparably damaged.

All my fault.

I gulp and sit down on the hard wooden chair across from Dr. Brasher's desk. My eyes veer away from the photo and right into a pink notebook. Hope wouldn't use a black and white speckled composition book, no. She made mom buy her a special English journal, with sparkly bling and a splashing dolphin. Sometimes she acted like she was nine years old.

My heart stutters. Why does Dr. Brasher have Hope's stuff? Did the judge send it here? My fingers itch to reach for it, but nothing I do seems to go right, so I force my hands into fists at my side.

This has to go right.

"Ah, I see you've caught me," Dr. Brasher says. "I was just studying up on your case, a little last minute maybe."

I start to speak, but I can't quite get words past the frog lodged in my throat. I cough to clear it and then force myself to croak a few words. "Why do you have Hope's journal and that photo?"

"Please," he says. "Sit down."

I do, but I can't help another pointed glance at the journal.

"Does it bother you that I have it?"

I stomp down on the surge of emotion. I just have to survive the next hour. "No, I'm just curious."

"I see in the file that you're only eleven months older than her. Irish twins, as it were."

I've explained this so many times, the words fall out without thought. "Since I was born in early fall and she came along the very next year at summer's end, we started kindergarten the same year."

"That's awfully close in age. Did you mind having a sister when you were little? Were you ever jealous of her?"

I don't snort at him, or tell him to look at the photo. I don't tell him that everyone was jealous of Hope. I don't tell him she ruined my life. I don't tell him I hated her sometimes. And I don't bother telling him I loved her, too. I loved her enough to keep giving and giving when all she did was take take take.

"Even if I was jealous, that's normal, right?" I ask. "Text-book, even. Half the kids in America are jealous of their new baby brother or sister."

He holds up the photo, one side of it flopping forward along the scotch tape fault line. "She looks a little different than you do."

Thank you Doctor Obvious. My brown curly hair looks nothing like Hope's long, blonde locks. Our eyes are the same shape, but different colors. My pale, lightly freckled arms and legs inspire vampire jokes galore. Her limbs are tanned and muscular from swimming. My angular face and bony body look even more gaunt when compared to her perfect curves.

I guess it's safe to say Hope didn't steal my looks, but she's taken most everything else I've wanted over the years, sometimes without even trying. When we were babies, she snatched pacifiers I wasn't ready to give up, my favorite stuffed animals, my snacks, and even my cutest clothing. As we grew, so too did the list in my head of stolen goods. I kept track of them all.

Not that I plan to confess that in an interrogation ordered by a judge.

"You're right. Only our face shapes look the same."

"Can you describe your relationship?"

I glance at the clock. "We've only got an hour, right?"

He smiles. "We have as long as you need, Angelica."

I shudder. "Don't call me that. My name is Lacy, okay?"

He makes a note on his yellow pad. It doesn't inspire confidence that he needs to write down my name, like he knows he won't remember it otherwise. Or maybe wanting to use a nickname tells him something about my brain. What does it tell him? I want to stand up and demand that he tell me. I want to know what's going to happen. I want to take everything back. Instead I clench my fists and try to school my face into a façade of calm.

I can't survive much more of this mock serenity. My head will explode. "For today we only have an hour, right?"

He nods. "I have another patient scheduled after you, but you can come back tomorrow and the next day, for as long as we need. We may be seeing each other a lot for the next few weeks."

My heart rate spikes. Weeks? I don't have that much time. Why would this take that long? I always finish tests in the first fifteen minutes. I write five page papers in half an hour. Why would it take that long to be evaluated?

Then it dawns on me. "Shrinks are all paid by the hour, right? So the more time it takes for you, the more money you make. Got to pay for that Porsche for the wife somehow, am I right?"

He shakes his head. "My wife drives a Subaru, and she paid for that herself. Would it interest you to know that psychiatrists are actually the worst paid doctors in America?"

I shrug. I don't really care much one way or another, but that might explain Melinda's dilemma.

"Speaking of," I say, and then stop. She asked me not to say anything, but maybe Dr. Brasher could do something about it. He might want to do something. It's not like I promised her I'd keep quiet. Things that can be fixed should be fixed. Before it's too late.

"Did you have something to tell me, Lacy?"

I look down at my feet and then back up to meet his eyes. "Do you like your secretary, Melinda?"

He raises just one eyebrow. "How is that related to psychiatrists being poorly paid?"

"I'll explain, but I need to know. Are you happy with her work?"

"Of course I am. I've been working with her for years. She's my secretary and also my office manager. She keeps things running."

"I get that you're not well paid, but she needs more money. She's got a son who's, well, I don't know exactly what his deal is, but if you don't give her that raise you can't afford, you might be looking for a new office manager."

Melinda's face had bleached white when we spoke earlier, but Dr. Brasher's doesn't grow pale. His cheeks flush crimson.

"Look, if it helps, you can write down that we spent as many hours as you want. I won't say a word." Happy shrink, better eval, right?

Dr. Brasher splutters. "I would never falsify my hours. And how could you know that Melinda needs money?"

I shrug. "I notice things." At least, now I do. "You only get one shot to get things right sometimes." Familiar tears well up in the back of my throat, my eyes misting. I take a big, ragged breath to head them off. "But whatever. You're the one with the fancy degrees, so I'm sure you know better than I do."

He steeples his hands in front of him and studies me. "Now you've gone all teenager on me, but you don't need to. I have an MD, yes, but I still appreciate insightful advice from any quadrant. Your file says you're in line to be Valedictorian, and I can see why. I feel as though I should set the record straight. For court-ordered evaluations, I'm paid on a flat fee basis."

Great, and my suggestion that he pad his bill makes me look like an idiotic teenager at best, a chronic liar at worst. Another spastic misstep. Heat floods my chest and spreads up to my cheeks. "That sucks for you, but it means you want to wrap this up as fast as you can, right? I'm on board with that."

"It takes as long as it takes," he practically growls. This could definitely be going better. He breathes in and out a few times before saying, "How did you feel about your little sister when you were growing up?"

"I loved her, of course. Everyone loves Hope. I'm pretty sure it's involuntary, like pupil dilation, or breathing."

Dr. Brasher scoffs. "Pupil dilation?"

I shrug. "I got tired of being the smart one sometimes, okay? It sucks, being the plain one, the boring one, but it's not like I could do much about it. If I bleached my hair and tried to swim or something, I'd have looked like a pathetic wannabe, a disappointing, washed-out clone. So I focused on my strengths and just tried to love her for hers."

"Did you ever like the same guys?"

My hands start to sweat. I didn't expect him to have her journal. I have no idea what it says in there. I don't like unknowns in mathematics, and I despise them in real life.

"Hope was on homecoming court, okay? She's swim team captain, so she meets a lot of jocks. The kind of guy who likes her is usually good looking, funny, smart, athletic, or popular."

Basically, anyone who's breathing.

"And what about you, Lacy? What kinds of guys like you?"

"Up until this year, the closest I got to having a guy's undivided attention was when I read Hemingway or Chaucer."

"What changed this year?" He steeples his hands again.

It's starting to annoy me. "I bet you've already read all about it."

"I don't know your side of things," Dr. Brasher says. "That's why you're here."

"If I walk you through what happened and you write your report, then we'll be done, right?"

He nods.

"Where should I start?"

"Where do you think it all started to go wrong?"

He already knows what happened and he's got Hope's journal, so he's probably figured out that it's all my fault.

Things went about as wrong as they could have gone. Fights. Missed school. Police. Drugs. Juvie. Possible expulsion. And the one bad thing no one ever seems to want to talk about.

I can barely breathe and I look away. Sniff and wipe my eyes.

She died.

The rest of the stuff doesn't even matter compared to that.

But looking back on all that mess, in the cluster my life has become, no one's asked for my side of the story. Not the judge, not a single teacher, not my friends, no one. It's like they're all afraid of the answer.

And maybe they should be.

It all started the day I met Mason. Is it ironic that the first truly great day of my life was probably also the very thing that set in motion the events leading up to the worst? Or does life always work like that? Mom lost Dad right after Hope was born. Maybe bad always nips at good's heels like a moronic, overeager puppy, shredding everything and peeing in the corner.

Dr. Brasher still stares at me expectantly and I realize I haven't spoken a word. "I guess it all started with Mason."

Dr. Brasher rifles through a pile of papers on his desk and then he looks back up at me. "Mason Montcellier?"

I nod my head, impressed when he pronounces the difficult last name correctly. "Yep."

"Why don't you tell me about him."

I bite my lip. I don't want to talk about Mason. It hurts. Not crippling pain, like when I think about her, but thinking about Mason hurts in a different way. Plus, I honestly don't even know how I feel anymore. I cared for Mason more than I thought possible, and now I have no idea how to feel about him. Do I love him? Do I blame him? Do I feel anything at all?

I clear my throat. "It was your typical story, I guess. Outrageously attractive boy meets nerdy girl. It was the 'happily ever after part' where things started to break down."

***Already Gone is available right now on all store fronts, or you can get it for free if you sign up for my newsletter, at www.BridgetEBakerWrites.com.

ACKNOWLEDGMENTS

My husband: you're the absolute best

My kids: you're my favorite, every single day (yes, all of you)

My readers: you inspire me and keep me going (and give me name ideas, too)

My editors: you make me look smarter than I really am—thank goodness

Bridget loves her husband (every day) and all five of her kids (most days). She's a lawyer, but does as little legal work as possible. She has three goofy horses, two scrappy cats, two adorable rabbits, one bouncy dog and backyard chickens. She hates Oxford commas, but she uses them to keep fans from complaining. She makes cookies waaaaay too often and believes they should be their own food group. In a possibly misguided attempt to keep from blowing up like a puffer fish, she kick boxes every day. So if you don't like her books, her kids, her pets, or her cookies, maybe don't tell her in person.

Suppressed (2)

Redeemed (3)

Renounced (4)

The Anchored Series:

Anchored (1)

Adrift (2)

Awoken (3—releasing July 15, 2021)

Capsized (4—releasing September 15, 2021)

A stand alone YA romantic suspense:

Already Gone

Children's Picture Book

Yuck! What's for Dinner?

www.ingramcontent.com/pod-product-compliance
Lightning Source LLC
Chambersburg PA
CBHW011213190726
48288CB00013B/3437